FAREWELL, MY DEUCE

The Reed Ferguson Mystery Series, Book 4

RENÉE PAWLISH

Farewell, My Deuce
A Reed Ferguson Mystery

First Digital Edition published by Llama Press
Copyright 2013 by Renée Pawlish

ACKNOWLEDGMENTS

The author gratefully acknowledges all those who helped in the writing of this book, especially: Beth Hecker, Beth Treat, and Janice Horne. If I've forgotten anyone, please accept my apologies.

CHAPTER ONE

"Deuce, put the gun down!"

"What's the matter, Reed?" Deuce stared at me over the barrel of the gun, his gray eyes wide. He squinted, gritted his teeth, and said, "I know what you're thinking. 'Did he fire six shots or only five?' Well, to tell you the truth, in all this excitement I kind of lost track myself. But being as this is a .44 Magnum, the most powerful handgun in the world, and would blow your head clean off, you've got to ask yourself one question: Do I feel lucky? Well, do ya, punk?"

I stared at Deuce, speechless. Now he thinks he's Clint Eastwood in *Dirty Harry*? "Don't point the gun at me!" I said, holding my hands up as if that could ward off a flying bullet.

"The gun's not loaded," Deuce said as he lowered his hand.

I stepped forward and carefully took the gun from him. "It doesn't matter," I growled. "It's not safe. You aim at the target and the target only, not at people."

"What if I'm a detective, like you, and I have to protect myself?" Deuce asked.

I took a deep breath and let it out slowly. *Patience, Reed, patience.* "Yes, in that situation, you would point at a person. But during target practice, you aim *only* at the target."

"Maybe you *were* the target," a relaxed, languid voice piped in. This was Ace, Deuce's big, but not any brighter, brother.

My eyes went from Ace to Deuce, dumbfounded. "You two are unbelievable. You can remember an entire scene from *Dirty Harry* but you can't remember the safety rules I just told you?"

"Ah, he was just having fun," Ace said.

I shook my head. I never thought I'd see the day when Deuce Smith shot a gun. And now I was sure I never wanted to see it again.

"C'mon, Reed, I'll stop goofing off," Deuce said. "I need my Magnum."

"It's not a Magnum, it's a Glock," I said, as I loaded the pistol. "I must've been crazy to bring you two here."

Here was the Silver Bullet Shooting Range. In truth, I'd only been to the range a half dozen times myself, when I needed to practice firing my gun, the Glock. My name is Reed Ferguson and I'm a private investigator. I love old detective novels and old movies, particularly film noir, with dark detectives and femme fatales. And although I hadn't been at the detecting business for too many years, you'd think I'd be a crack shot with a gun. In truth, I really didn't want to shoot anyone, so I preferred not to carry a gun in the first place. But as my cases have put me in increasingly dangerous situations, I've felt compelled to carry my gun more often. And I figured if I was going to carry a gun, I'd better be able to use it properly. And maybe hit more than the broad side of my office building.

"Hurry up, Reed," Deuce said, dancing from foot to foot. "I gotta practice. I may need to protect myself."

I stared at the two guys before me, both tall with dirty blond hair and blank gray eyes. Ace and Deuce Smith are my rather slow, very naïve neighbors, whom I affectionately referred to as The Goofball Brothers. Although neither was anywhere close to what you'd call high IQ, they were my friends. We hung out, played pool and watched movies, and on occasion they'd helped with my investigations. Deuce had even been beaten up by someone trying to intimidate me. His dream has been to use a gun, and I finally let him talk me into bringing him to the shooting range. It was a beautiful fall Friday evening in early October; I should've been out enjoying it. As I said before, I must've been crazy.

"Okay, here you go." I carefully handed the Glock to Deuce.

"Yeah," Deuce said, slowing turning toward the target. "Okay, punk." He spread his legs, squared his shoulders, and fashioned a snarl on his face. Then he stretched his arms out. He was trying so hard to look tough, but his hands shook.

"Aim and shoot," Ace said.

"Don't rush me." Deuce closed one eye, sighted down the barrel, and gently squeezed the trigger, just like I'd shown him.

Bang!

Deuce whooped in a high-pitched voice and jumped back. I had *not* shown him that.

"That was so cool!" he shouted.

I glanced around. A burly guy in the next stall over glared at us, then shook his head. I nodded at him. He muttered something that I, fortunately I expect, couldn't hear through my earplugs.

"Just keep shooting," I said, nudging Deuce back into place in front of the counter.

Deuce aimed at the target and pulled the trigger again. This time, he managed to keep his excitement under check and he emptied the gun.

"How'd I do?" he asked when he'd finished.

"Let's see."

I pushed the button that controlled the target retriever, and the paper target zoomed back on its track to us. As it got closer, I shuddered. The target stopped a few feet from us, swaying slightly.

"Where are the holes?" Deuce asked, dumbfounded. The black paper with a body-shaped outline was in pristine condition.

"I think you missed the target," Ace snickered.

"I didn't hit it once?" Deuce asked.

"No, you didn't," I said. Ace howled with laughter.

Deuce plopped the gun on the counter and whirled around. "See if you can do better," he said as he pushed Ace forward.

"No problem." Ace grabbed the gun and pointed at the target.

"Uh, Ace," I said.

"Don't stop me," Ace said, squinting an eye shut. He sucked in a breath and held it, liked I'd instructed, then pulled the trigger.

Click.

Ace paused, stared at the gun, then at me.

"You need bullets," I said.

Ace smiled sheepishly. "Yeah, right."

"And we need to put the target back in place."

"I could've hit it if it was that close," Deuce said.

Ace punched Deuce. "Put the target back and I'll hit it."

I pressed the button and the target chugged back down the track, fifteen yards from us. There wasn't a need to replace it, since it was unblemished. Then I loaded the Glock and handed it to Ace.

"Try again."

Ace took the gun, aimed and fired off all fifteen rounds. When he'd finished, Deuce peered over his shoulder.

"How'd he do?" Deuce asked.

4

I pressed the target retrieval button again and brought the target back. We all stared at it.

"Still no holes in it," Ace said.

I nodded. "I think you guys need a bit more practice."

"Let's see you try it," Deuce nudged me.

"Okay." In truth, I hadn't been practicing much at all, but I figured I could at least hit the target. I loaded the gun again, got into position, sucked in a breath, aimed and fired. I repeated the process until I'd emptied the gun.

"Let's see the target now," the Goofball Brothers chimed.

I grinned as the target made its way back toward us. As it drew near, I noticed I hadn't embarrassed myself too much. I'd actually managed to hit all my shots inside the outline of the body. Good thing, since the Goofball Brothers thought I was an ace private eye.

"Wow, you're good," Ace said, with awe in his voice.

I hoped he didn't see the target of the guy next to us. As his black paper target came back, the holes were all in a tight little circle in the center of the body outline.

"My turn," Deuce said.

And so went the next hour. The Brothers got a bit better; by the end they'd both managed to actually hit the paper, and I was thoroughly exhausted from trying to manage the two of them.

"How about some pool?" I finally asked. "I told Willie we might go to B 52's for a while."

B 52's is the bar where we liked to hang out and Willie Rhoden is our neighbor. Her real name is Willimena, she's a nurse, and after many attempts on my part, she'd finally agreed to a date with me. It had gone well enough that she'd agreed to another date. And then another. I was beginning to wonder if I could call her my girlfriend...

"Yeah, let's go," Ace said. "This was fun, but I'd rather play pool."

"This was awesome," Deuce said as he watched me put the Glock back in its case. "Reed, I think I've got the hang of it." He nodded knowingly. "I can protect myself, and when I help you, I should carry a gun."

Oh, wouldn't *that* be great.

———

"How did it go?" Willie asked later.

"I wouldn't want either of them to protect and serve," I said as I brought a couple of Fat Tires from the bar. "My mother could shoot better than them."

"Has she ever –" She stopped when she saw me roll my eyes. "No, of course not."

Willie hadn't had the fortune of meeting my doting, worrying mother. But she'd heard me talk about my mother...a lot. My mother was sweet and as naïve as the Goofball Brothers. She'd never laid eyes on a gun, and she'd be shocked that I owned one, let alone that I could actually shoot it.

"Hey, Willie, did you hear about how I did?" Ace asked as he leaned over the pool table, preparing for a difficult shot. "I was pretty good."

"I heard that," she said, her green eyes twinkling humorously. She definitely had a soft spot for the Goofball Brothers, and they loved her.

"Pretty good...right," Deuce said from across the table.

"I was." Ace sunk the five-ball in the corner pocket.

"How did he make that?" I muttered, shaking my head. The Brothers combined could barely add two and two, and they were terrible on the shooting range, but both could play pool like Minnesota Fats. Go figure.

We watched them for a few minutes, enjoying the 80's music that pumped from hidden speakers in the ceiling. I loved B 52's. What was once a warehouse was now a pool hall decorated with old plane propellers and advertisements from the 1940s and '50s. It reminded me of the film noir movies that I was such a fan of, a long-gone era that I loved.

"Your turn." Deuce came up and handed a pool cue to Willie.

"Deuce, you know I'm not any good," Willie laughed.

"Come on. I'll go easy on you," Deuce said.

They started playing, Ace and Deuce chattering at Willie as they instructed her on the finer points of the game. The game finished, and while Ace showed Willie how to set up a particular shot, Deuce walked over.

"The range was fun," he said over Depeche Mode singing *People Are People*.

"Yeah, it was," I said. My nerves had settled so I could agree.

"Hey, Reed, I was going to ask you about something about rigging."

"You interested in sailing?"

"Huh?" He looked at me blankly, a typical Goofball Brothers expression.

"Deuce, come on, it's your turn," Ace hollered at him.

"Oh right." He took a quick swig of beer. "Never mind." He went to the table and started playing again.

What does Deuce want to know about sailing, I thought. I'd talked to them some about my college days at Harvard. I'd been a political science major and intended to study law, but, really, I majored in sailing and was part of the Crimson team. Initially I was the crew, but my senior year I skippered a number of races, even winning the Hood Trophy with my partner and then-girlfriend, Alicia Ferrigam. I hadn't thought of her in years. She'd tie up her brown hair when she sailed, and she'd smile in a mischievous way. And she was competitive...I tended not to give up on things and that was in part because she drove me to win.

"What's that look on your face?" Willie asked as she reached for her beer.

I came out of my reverie. "Nothing, just thinking about sailing."

"Sailing?"

"Yeah, I used to sail some, in college."

"The things I learn about you," she said.

"I'm not just a great detective, I'm multilayered," I smiled.

"Reed," she murmured into my ear.

"Uh huh," I said as I watched Ace try a difficult shot.

"Let's go home so I can peel off some of those layers."

"Okay," I said, watching the game.

"Do you have an extra toothbrush?"

"You need a new one? We can stop at the store on the way home."

"Reed." Willie snuggled closer to me. "Are the Goofball Brothers wearing off on you?"

"What do you mean? I –" Then it dawned on me what Willie meant. I stared at her, then grinned. "Yeah, I've got an extra toothbrush."

"Hey, guys," Willie called to Ace and Deuce. "We're leaving. You two have fun." Then she took my hand and led me out of the bar.

CHAPTER TWO

Hours later, Humphrey Bogart's voice woke me out of a dead sleep. "Such a lot of guns around town, and so few brains." It was a line from *The Big Sleep*, one of my favorite film noir movies, and I'd made it my ringtone.

I fumbled for the phone. "Hello?" I mumbled.

"Reed, it's Ace."

"Ace, what time is it?"

"Almost six."

I sat up and rubbed my eyes. Pale yellow light filtered through the cracks of the window blinds.

"It's Saturday, Ace," I said. "Why are you calling so early?"

"It's Deuce. He's missing."

I rubbed a hand over my face. "What do you mean he's missing?"

"Who is it?" Willie rolled over and yawned. "It's my day off."

She opened one eye and cocked her head, listening. I stared at her for a moment, then let my eyes wander around my bedroom. Yep, it was my bedroom. I closed my eyes and opened them again. Willie smiled at me. Yep, she was still here. *How about that?*

"Reed, Deuce isn't here," Ace said with more force in his voice.

I tore my eyes away from Willie. "Just because Deuce isn't there doesn't mean he's missing. Maybe he got up early and went somewhere."

"No, he didn't," Ace said. "When we left the bar last night, Deuce got a call. Then he said he had to meet someone and that he'd see me at home. But he never came home."

"Are you sure?"

"Yes. When I got home, I watched some TV and I fell asleep on the couch. If Deuce came home, he would've woke me up."

"There's no way he could've snuck in and you slept through it?"

"I don't think so. Besides, why would he sneak in the house?"

I sighed. "I don't know. I'm going over all the possibilities."

"Maybe he's got a girlfriend," Willie whispered.

Really? I mouthed at her. *Deuce?*

She shrugged. "It's possible."

Yeah, and I'm Humphrey Bogart, I thought.

"Does Deuce have a girlfriend?" I asked Ace. Stranger things have happened.

"Huh?" Ace said.

"Is Deuce dating anyone? And he slept at her house? Maybe that's who called him."

A long pause ensued.

"Ace?"

"I don't think Deuce has a girlfriend," Ace finally said. "He'd tell me that."

I had to agree. The Brothers were extremely close, and I couldn't see them keeping secrets from each other.

"Is there anyone else he could've stayed with last night?"

I could hear Ace grinding his teeth. "I don't think so."

"What about Bob? Could he have gone to Bob's?"

Bob Smith was Ace and Deuce's older brother. Bob was lucky in two respects: his father had discovered his love of poker only after Bob was born, so he'd gotten a normal name – plus, apparently all the brains for the family. He was an EMT and a few years earlier he'd moved back to Denver from the East Coast so he could keep an eye out on his dimwitted brothers.

"But why wouldn't Deuce tell me he was going to Bob's? He should've called," Ace said, now clearly convinced that Deuce had indeed spent the night at Bob's house. "I can't believe he didn't tell me."

"Ace, we don't know if he went to Bob's," I said. "It was just a thought." I swung my legs over the side of the bed. "Tell you what. You call Bob and see if Deuce is there. Then let me know."

Ace agreed and hung up. I figured I would get a call back with a negative. Ace was right; there was no way Deuce would spend the night at Bob's and not tell him.

"Deuce never came home?" Willie asked.

I glanced over my shoulder at her. Her short blond hair was tussled, she had a beguiling smile on her face, and the sheets barely covered her. I turned around and gave her a kiss.

"No, Deuce didn't come home," I replied. I dropped the phone and ran my hands under the sheets. More skin.

"You think something's wrong?"

"I doubt it. It's a case of Goofball Brother confusion. Nothing to worry about." My hands explored her body. "Last night was great."

"Hmm," she said.

"Let's spend the day in bed."

"Reed!" Willie smacked my arm. "What about Ace?"

"Hey, the Goofball Brothers are great. Just not too bright."

"That's not what I mean."

"Okay." I kissed her neck. "I think we should continue what we started last night."

My cell phone rang. And my kisses continued.

"Reed." Willie giggled as she grabbed my phone and handed it to me.

I stopped. "Way to kill a mood."

She smirked at me as I put the phone to my ear.

"He's not at Bob's," Ace said. "Bob hasn't heard from him since last week. Reed, something's wrong."

I sighed. "Okay, I'll be right down."

"Bob's coming over."

I hung up. "Bob's coming over. He can handle things, don't you think?" I stared at Willie.

"Reed, you need to go help Ace."

"I'm sure it's nothing." I kissed her shoulder. "Just a misunderstanding."

"Reed, what about Ace?"

I sat back and sighed. "Whatever Deuce is up to, it better be good."

"I'll come down, too." Willie got up and went into the bathroom.

"Oh boy, we'll have a party." I crawled off the bed and followed her. "How about a quick shower?"

The door closed in my face. It couldn't hurt to try, could it?

CHAPTER THREE

Ace and Deuce owned the condo below me. We live in Uptown, immediately east of downtown Denver. It's a great old neighborhood, with a mix of Victorian and Queen Anne homes, high-rise apartments, lofts and condos. There's no way the Brothers could afford this kind of a place on their own; I'm pretty sure their parents help out. When Willie and I walked in, Ace was in the kitchen, making coffee.

"Bob will be here soon," he said as he handed me a cup. Worry lines creased his normally innocent face. "Do you want something to eat?" He rummaged in a cupboard and pulled out a box of Cheerios. "Deuce always cooks breakfast, not me."

I held up my cup. "Coffee's fine."

"Ace, I'm sure Deuce is fine," Willie said as she waited for Ace to pour her a cup. "He was probably just too tired to come home so he crashed at his friend's house."

"What friend?" Ace asked.

"The one he went to see after he left you," she said.

Ace nodded, but he wasn't convinced. "I dunno..."

The front door opened. "Ace?" a deep voice called. A

moment later, Bob Smith appeared in the kitchen doorway. Bob was the mirror image of his brothers; only the wrinkles at the corners of his eyes betrayed the fact that he was older.

"Bob!" Ace breathed a sigh of relief. "I don't know what to do..." His voice cracked.

"Hey," Bob put a hand on Ace's shoulder and comforted him, then nodded to Willie and me. "So what's going on? I couldn't follow everything you were saying on the phone."

"Deuce didn't come home last night," Ace said simply. He began pacing back and forth between the refrigerator and the stove. Three paces, turn. Three paces, turn.

"Reed, can you fill me in?" Bob said as he fixed himself a cup of coffee.

"You know about as much as we do," I said. I turned to Ace. "Tell Bob everything you told me."

Ace continued pacing as he relayed his conversation with me.

Bob leaned against the counter and sipped his coffee, listening intently. "It's not like Deuce to not come home, and certainly not to call," he said when Ace finished.

"Let's go over this again," I said. "Ace, you said that when you and Deuce left B 52's, Deuce got a phone call and said he had to meet someone."

"That's right," Ace said.

"Did you hear the person's voice on the phone? Anything that would tell you if it was a man or woman?"

"No. I wasn't that close to him."

"What do you remember of the conversation?" I asked. "What exactly did Deuce say?"

Ace stood still for a moment and stared at the ceiling, thinking. "I think he said 'Hey, man,' and then he said, 'Where are you?' Then he said 'Right now?' and then 'Okay, I can meet you there,' and 'I won't'. After that, he hung up."

"That's amazing recall." I grabbed a piece of paper and pen from the counter and jotted it all down. "Would you say Deuce was surprised that this person wanted to meet right then?"

Ace nodded his head vigorously. "Yes. We didn't leave B 52's until it closed."

That would've been one a.m. Definitely an odd time to go meet someone.

"Do you remember what Deuce said to you when he hung up?" This from Bob.

"He said he had to go," Ace said.

"That's all?" I pushed. "You sure he didn't say anything else?"

Ace chewed his lip. "No, just 'I gotta go'."

"Was he apprehensive?" I asked. Ace stared at me blankly. I tried again. "Was he nervous? Seemed like he didn't want to go?"

"Oh," Ace nodded. "Yeah, now that you're asking, I think he did seem a little...apprehensive."

"So it wasn't a friend he met," Bob concluded.

"Probably not," I said. I continued with Ace. "Did you ask him where he was going?"

"Sure. He said 'I can't tell you' and then he walked off down the street."

"So you *walked* to B 52's last night?" I confirmed. That wasn't unusual because the bar is close to where we live, and last night the weather was perfect, comfortably cool without a cloud in the sky.

"Uh huh," Ace said.

"Is Deuce's truck parked outside now?" I asked.

Ace raised his eyebrows. "I don't know. I didn't think to look."

Bob went to the kitchen window and looked out into the back yard. There was a garage and one parking space for each unit. Ace parked his Subaru in the garage, and Deuce parked his old Chevy truck in his allotted space next to the building.

"I can't see if it's there," Bob said.

"Let's go check," I said, standing up. "Ace, do you have a set of spare keys?"

"Sure, why?"

"If it's there, I want to look inside."

"Ah," Ace said. "So you can look for clues."

I smiled. "Right."

Ace rummaged in a drawer and produced a key ring with a few keys on it. "It's this one," he said, handing it to me.

I took it and we all traipsed out the back door, down the stairs, and around the side of the building.

"There's his truck," I said.

Deuce's Chevy was sitting in his parking space. I walked around it and tried the doors. "It's locked." I used the key to open the driver's side door and we all looked inside.

"Not much here," I said. An empty Starbucks mug sat in the console between the seats. Spare change was thrown in a cubbyhole. Napkins and receipts lay strewn on the passenger seat. I grabbed the receipts. "McDonald's. A gas station. Home Depot. A list of some construction companies: T. F. Byers Construction, Pearson Construction, and a couple more. Mean anything to anyone?"

"Deuce works in construction," Bob said. "He's probably worked with those companies."

"Okay." I crouched down and poked around under the seats. "Nothing," I finally said, leaning against the car door. "But then, I'm not sure what I expected to find."

"Why would Deuce be so mysterious about where he was going?" Willie asked as we headed back inside. "That doesn't sound like him at all."

"He usually can't shut up," Ace said. Spoken like a brother.

"You think whoever called Deuce asked him not to say anything?" Bob said. "And that's why Deuce said 'I won't'."

"Makes sense to me," I said.

Once we were back in the kitchen, Bob turned to Ace. "Did he have plans today? Were you guys going anywhere?"

"No," Ace said. "I was going to go by work and bring a movie home for tonight, but I don't think Deuce was planning on doing anything." Ace worked at a nearby Blockbuster; he had been promoted to assistant manager, and was thriving with the extra responsibility. We all hoped the experience would help him, in case the store closed and he had to find work elsewhere.

Something suddenly occurred to me. "Did you try calling Deuce?"

Ace slapped a hand to his head. "Duh," he said to himself.

I felt like an idiot, too. I'd just assumed that Ace would try that, and that was my mistake. With the Goofball Brothers, you can't assume anything.

Ace picked up his cell phone and dialed Deuce's number. "It's his voicemail," Ace said after a moment.

"Ask him to call you as soon as he gets the message," Bob instructed him.

Ace did and hung up. "Now what?"

"Let's check his room," I said. "Maybe we'll find something that'll help us."

Once again we left the kitchen and headed down a short hallway and into Deuce's room. His dresser held a flat screen TV, and stacks of comic books were strewn about the floor. A Spiderman poster was pinned to the light blue wall above the queen-sized bed.

"I didn't know he liked comics," I said.

"He doesn't tell people because he doesn't want them to think he's a nerd," Ace said.

Bob suppressed a smile. "Spidy's his favorite."

Everyone gazed expectantly at me. The great detective needs to start detecting. I looked around. Except for the comics, the room was surprisingly neat. No clothes on the floor, no dust on the furniture. And the bed was made.

"Surprisingly neat room," I muttered.

Ace threw me a half-smile. "Mom told us we needed to clean up."

Bob hid another smile. "You can look through everything," he said, giving me permission to delve into the dresser drawers and closet.

"Someone check the closet," I said as I moved to the dresser. "See if there's anything unusual."

"Like what?" Ace asked.

"How would I know?" I shrugged.

"Aren't you the detective?" Bob said.

"It's not as exciting as you'd think. It's a lot of..." I glanced around. "This."

I opened all the drawers and looked inside. Shirts, underwear, and socks neatly stored in the drawers. I ran my hands through it all. "This is a bust," I said, then stopped. "What's this?"

A pile of money jutted out from beneath his socks. I picked them up and counted them, all twenties.

"There's over five hundred dollars here," I said.

Bob came over, staring at the money. "Why would he have that much cash lying around?" he asked, turning to Ace.

Ace shrugged. "I don't know. He never said anything to me about extra money."

"Is he saving for something?" Willie asked.

"I don't think so," Ace said. "And if he was, I don't know why he'd keep it here instead of in the bank."

I put the money back and turned around. "Anything else unusual?"

"No, not a thing," Bob said as he shut the closet door.

Willie and Ace shook their heads.

"So, Deuce has a lot of money in his sock drawer, and that's it," I recapped as we went into the living room.

"What now?" Willie asked. "Should we call the police?"

I shook my head. "They won't do anything for twenty-four hours. But maybe we should try the hospitals, in case he got hurt."

"You think he was in an accident?" Ace's jaw dropped.

"I doubt it," Bob said. "I'm sure Deuce will show up and we'll find out this was all a big mix-up, but we should check just in case." He spoke calmly but the worry in his eyes betrayed him.

"I can help with that," Willie said. "Ace, can you log me onto your computer so I can look up the hospital phone numbers?"

Ace went with Willie to a desk in the corner of the room. "Should I call Mom and Dad?" Ace asked as he typed at the keyboard.

Bob pursed his lips. "No, let's wait a bit. I don't want to worry them needlessly. Besides," he put a hand on Ace's shoulder and squeezed. "I'm sure Deuce will come home soon, and he'll be apologizing for getting us all worried."

"I hope so," Ace said.

"Let's backtrack again," I said, looking at the notes I'd written. "Ace, did you notice anyone unusual at the bar? Did anyone follow you home?"

Ace thought for a moment. "No, but I wasn't paying attention."

"Maybe Deuce went back to the bar," I said. "I'll check with the staff later today. Ace, why don't you stay here and help Willie call the hospitals and I'll try to track down who called Deuce."

"I'll call his friends, too, see if anyone's heard from him," Bob said.

"Good idea," I agreed.

I pulled out my phone and found Deuce's number. "This is still his number, right?" I showed it to Ace.

"Yeah," Ace said.

"Who's your carrier?"

"Verizon."

"You can find out who called him?" Bob asked, incredulous.

"I can't," I said. "But I know someone who can."

CHAPTER FOUR

"So Deuce is missing," Cal Whitmore said as he let me into his house.

Most great detectives have a sidekick. Sherlock Holmes had Dr. Watson. Nero Wolfe had Archie Goodwin. I had my best friend, Cal. I'd known him since we were kids, where we'd been inseparable. We'd even attended Harvard together, although his grades were much better than mine. I goofed around and my grades suffered. He goofed around and still got straight A's. He was as smart as anyone I knew, but at the same time, he couldn't butter bread. Brilliant, but no common sense.

"Yeah, and I need you to find a phone number," I said as I followed Cal through a sparsely furnished living room and down a hallway to his home office.

Cal was a computer genius and his office reflected this. Multiple computers and monitors filled his oversized desk. He listened to music on state-of-the-art speakers and watched DVDs on a 30-inch monitor. Piles of papers, books, manuals, boxes of old disks, cords, and CDs were stacked against the walls. At any given time, at least a few dishes, glasses, soda cans, or beer bottles were strewn about the room. I shuddered when I thought of what science project might be growing in them.

"A phone number should be easy to find," Cal said, settling his lanky frame into a leather chair. "Let me finish up here..." His hands flew across the keyboard for a second and then he turned to me. Cal's specialty was computer viruses and virus protection, and his skills were highly sought after. He was involved with organizations and people that most of us knew nothing about, and he could hack into almost any system, even the Pentagon's. It's why he had a secluded home outside of Pine Junction, west of downtown Denver. He lived a quiet, reclusive life, rarely leaving his home. And he covered his tracks so well, it's almost as if he didn't exist.

"I've got Deuce's cell phone number," I said, handing Cal a piece of paper. "His carrier is Verizon. A little after one a.m. this morning Deuce received a phone call. I want to know who called him, where this person lives, and anything else we can find out about this person."

"Piece of cake." His brown eyes glinted and he started humming as he set to work. Tap, tap, tap. When Cal worked at the keyboard it was as if he was effortlessly playing a piano concerto. In seconds he said, "Okay, I've got Deuce's cell phone records."

I pulled up a folding chair and gazed at the computer screen. "That was fast."

Cal snorted. "C'mon, that was easy."

On the screen were Deuce's phone records.

"That's great," I said.

Cal manipulated the mouse for a second, then pointed at the monitor. "Here's the list of calls Deuce received in the last twenty-four hours."

I scooted my chair closer and stared at the monitor. Deuce had received six calls since noon on Friday.

"Recognize any of them?" Cal asked.

"This one is Ace," I said, pointing to a number. "That was this morning."

"What time was the call you're wondering about?"

"One a.m. or so."

"Right here." Cal highlighted part of the screen with the mouse. "The call lasted thirty-two seconds. Here's the number that called Deuce."

Cal rattled it off and I jotted it down, along with the other numbers.

"Let me call it," I said, grabbing my phone and dialing the number. It rang for a moment and then a generic message came on. "No name." I set the phone down. "Can you figure out who owns this number?"

Cal looked at me askance. "Does the pope live in Rome?"

"Technically, he lives in Vatican City."

"Whatever," Cal said. "Give me a minute."

"And can we listen to any messages left on his phone?"

Cal nodded and he set to work again. The screen flickered as windows popped up and closed with dizzying speed.

"How are things with you and Willie?" he asked, not taking his eyes off the screen. I grinned. He stopped and turned to me. "What?"

"She spent the night last night."

"No kidding?"

"Hey, keep working." I waved at the screen.

"Sorry." Cal focused again, but a smile spread across his face. "You and Wille...about time."

"Yeah, but I haven't had a chance to savor it." I'd hardly had time to think about the last twelve hours because of Deuce. "I'll tell you what, if this is some practical joke that Deuce is playing..."

"You think he'd do that?"

I frowned. "No, that's the problem. He tells Ace everything." I stood up, irritated. "I'm going to get a drink," I said. "You want anything?"

Cal barely shook his head as he declined. He was in the zone, murmuring as he worked. I left him alone and wandered into the kitchen, searching for something with caffeine in it. I grabbed a Coke from the refrigerator, opened it and took a long swig while I gazed out the kitchen window. Cal's house was built on a gentle slope that afforded gorgeous views of the Rocky Mountains. On a distant ridge the sun hit a green and gold grove of aspen, and it was like looking at a painting. Sadly, a sight like this one was wasted on Cal because he was almost always in front of his computer. I smiled to myself and went back to the office.

"...Vatican City...knew what I meant," Cal muttered under his breath as I sat back down.

"Let it go, big guy," I said, punching his arm.

"Uh huh. I should quit helping you out."

"Aw, you love it."

"As long as you don't drag me out of this house to help you."

"It's good for you," I said. Somehow I'd managed to get Cal's assistance on a couple of my cases, assistance that required him to leave the safety of his house.

Cal's lips curled into a smile.

"Admit it," I ordered.

Cal laughed. "Okay, it was kind of fun. But not again. And..." he paused for effect. "There was only one message on his phone, from Ace, left this morning. And here's the name registered to the number that called Deuce at one a.m. Gary Granderson. Here." Cal handed me a piece of paper. "Now you know what he looks like."

"How'd you get that?" I asked.

"I found his driver's license photo and printed it." He shrugged. "Don't ask how."

I studied the picture. Gary stared with cold blue eyes at the camera, no smile, trying to appear tough. It reminded me of a mug shot. His long brown hair was thinning on top, and he weighed 160 at the time the license was issued. "So Gary, what were you doing calling Deuce at one in the morning?"

"Unless someone else used Gary's phone to call Deuce."

I raised an eyebrow at him. "Highly unlikely, don't you think?"

"True."

"What can you tell me about Gary?"

"He's twenty-eight, never married, no kids. High school diploma. Here's his address." Cal highlighted a portion of the monitor.

"He lives off of Evans and Santa Fe, west of the DU campus," I said, referring to the University of Denver. "What else can you tell me about him?"

"Does he have a record, that kind of thing?"

"Yes."

Cal's fingers flew over the keyboard. "He had a DUI two years ago, he's had a couple of speeding tickets, and he was arrested for assault three years ago. He works at Criss Cross Construction."

"That was a great movie," I said as I continued jotting notes.

"What?"

"*Criss Cross*. It's a movie starring Burt Lancaster, and it was Tony Curtis' screen debut."

"And one of your favorite noir, right?" Cal and I'd been friends since grade school and he knew of my love of all things film noir.

"It's a classic," I said. "Lancaster gets involved in a love triangle, then commits a robbery and gets shafted by his partners."

"He gets criss-crossed," Cal laughed.

"Yeah," I said. I sat back in my chair. "Deuce works in construction."

"How much you want to bet Gary and Deuce work together?"

I shook my head. "I won't take that bet."

"What do you think Gary wanted with Deuce?"

"Good question," I said.

"You think Deuce is in real trouble?"

"I don't know." I sighed. "It's not like him to up and leave and not tell anyone. But it's not like him to get into trouble, either."

"You're really worried about him, aren't you?"

I met Cal's gaze. "Yeah, I guess I am." I realized that even though I teased the Goofball Brothers, we'd become good friends, and I didn't want to see anything bad happen to them.

"I'm here to help," Cal said.

"You already have," I said, tapping my notes. "I think it's time for me to pay Gary a visit and find out why he called Deuce."

"It's about lunchtime," Cal said. "You want something to eat? I've got leftovers."

I glanced at a plate of dried-out bread crusts. "Thanks, but I'll get a bite somewhere."

"Suit yourself." Cal turned back to the computer. "Let me know when you find Deuce. And tell your mom hello from me." My mom loves Cal, and she treats him almost like a son.

"I will," I said and left him to his work.

CHAPTER FIVE

As I headed down Highway 285 back toward Denver, I called Ace.

"Hey, hear anything from Deuce?" I asked, even though I knew Ace would've called if he'd heard from his younger brother.

"No, Reed. Not a word. Willie and Bob called all the hospitals in the area but Deuce isn't at any of them."

"That's good, at least he's not hurt." Granted, Deuce could be hurt, or worse, somewhere else, but why mention that to Ace? "Have any of his friends heard from him or know where he might be?"

"No one's talked to him in a few days," Ace said. "What did you find out?"

"A guy named Gary Granderson called Deuce after you guys left the bar," I said. "Have you ever heard Deuce mention him?"

"I don't think so," Ace said slowly.

"Next question: where does Deuce work?"

"Criss Cross Construction."

Bingo. "Gary and Deuce work together," I said.

"So why would Gary call Deuce so late?"

"I'm on my way to Gary's now, to ask him that very thing."

"I hope he knows something," Ace said. "I'm really getting worried."

Me, too, but I didn't say so. "I'm sure Deuce is fine. Maybe he went over to Gary's to have a few more drinks and he's too hung over to come home."

"Yeah, maybe." Ace wasn't convinced. Neither he nor Deuce was a big drinker.

"Are Willie and Bob still there?"

"Bob had to go home and get ready for work, but Willie's still here."

"That's nice of her to stay."

"Yeah," he said. Relief laced his voice. He clearly didn't want to be alone.

"Can I talk to her?"

I heard Ace mumbling something and then Willie's voice burst through the phone. "Hey, handsome, what's going on?" she asked, trying for cheery but not quite succeeding.

"I'm still out detecting." I filled her in on everything.

"Let's hope Gary can tell us what's going on," she said when I'd finished, "and where Deuce is."

"That would be good."

"What else can I do?"

I thought for a moment. "Nothing, really. Keep Ace company if he still wants it."

"I'll stay," she said. "We've been watching an Arnold Schwarzenegger movie, trying to keep from worrying." She lowered her voice. "He doesn't know what to do without Deuce around."

"If anything would help, it'd be Arnold." Schwarzenegger was Ace's favorite actor.

"Are you coming back after you see Gary?"

"I want to go by B 52's and see if anyone saw him come back."

"Will they be open?"

"Yes. It's Saturday and there's a Rockies game tonight, so they'll be open." B 52's was located near Coors Field, where the Colorado Rockies baseball team played, and many fans stopped at the bar before and after games. "I'll head home after that."

"How about we order a pizza, and Ace can join us if he wants."

"Works for me," I said.

I hung up and turned on the radio. I love 80's music, and The Smiths, a great British alternative rock band, are one of my favorites. I had their singles collection loaded up, and while "Heaven Knows I'm Miserable Now" played, my mind wandered over what I'd found out, which was next to nothing. I was feeling a little miserable myself, at my lack of progress. I tried to enjoy the drive – fall in the mountains of Colorado is spectacular, with golden aspen groves dotting the hillsides – but my concern for Deuce overshadowed that.

I drove out of the foothills and stayed on Highway 285, a north-south highway that actually meandered east and west through Denver. I exited on Federal, drove north to Evans, and then east. Gary Granderson lived in an older Denver neighborhood that was an eclectic mix of homes, some nicely kept up, others shabbier. It was a quarter past two when I turned onto Acoma Street. The houses were small one-story, most with small lawns and alley garages. And right in the middle of the street sat a rundown duplex. The two units were connected by two single-car garages that shared a driveway. Tan paint peeled from the siding and faded sheer curtains covered the front window of the south unit, where Gary lived. I parked my 4Runner on the street and walked past a dried-out lawn to the front porch. I rang the bell and waited. It couldn't have been a better day, the air warm but not stifling, and I wondered if maybe Gary was out enjoying it. After a minute, I pushed the button again, listening for a bell sound. Nothing. I banged on an aluminum door that had jagged rips in the screen. A moment later I heard footsteps and then the inner door opened.

"Yeah?" The man in front of me was average height, but muscles bulged through a tee shirt stained with grease spots and dirt. And, unlike the driver's license photo, this man had a shaved head. Colorful tattoos covered his arms, starting at his wrists and disappearing under his shirtsleeves.

"Gary?"

"Yeah?" he repeated. It came out in a rush, as if he was irritated, in a hurry to get back to the college football game that I could hear playing in the other room.

"My name is Reed Ferguson and I'm a friend of Deuce Smith." Gary stared at me through the screen. The smell of cigarette smoke and beer lingered in the air. "You know Deuce, right?"

"Don't think I do," he said. The television volume in the other room grew louder, crowd noise, and Gary glanced over his shoulder.

I eyed him for a second. "You work with him."

"It's a big company." Gary ran a hand over his bare skull. "Maybe he's on a different job than me."

"You know him." I pulled open the screen door. "You've even called him."

Gary scratched his stomach as he surveyed me. "Maybe I've seen him around. Maybe I've called him. So?"

"Deuce went out to play pool last night and he never came home. You talked to him last night and I'm wondering if you know where he went or what might have happened to him."

Something flashed in his eyes, a wariness. "I didn't talk to him," he said, a bit too quickly.

"Yes, you did. You called him. Deuce's brother was with him, and he overheard the call."

"Wait a minute." He took a step back, puzzled, but also cautious. "I didn't call Deuce last night."

I pressed him hard. "You called him at about one this morning."

"No, I didn't." His face turned to stone. "I hardly know him."

"I have Deuce's phone records. He received a call from you at about one."

Gary stared at me.

"Trying to think of a lie?" I finally asked.

"How do you have his phone records? You the cops or something?"

"I'm his friend, but I'm also a private investigator."

"No way you could get his phone records legally."

"How I got them doesn't matter," I said, hoping to deflect his very astute comment. "I'm just trying to find Deuce. It's not like him to not tell anyone where he went."

"Listen, pal." Gary straightened up and crossed his arms, challenging. "I didn't call Deuce last night and I haven't seen him in I don't know how long. I don't know where he is, either."

Something Cal said popped into my brain. I leaned against the screen, casually, so he'd know I wasn't intimidated. "Did you loan your phone to anyone?"

"Of course not," he snapped.

"Then how do you explain your number showing up on Deuce's phone?"

"I don't know and I don't care."

"How about letting me see your phone?"

"What for?" he asked, an edge in his voice.

"So I can see the phone history," I said, even though I knew he could've deleted Deuce's number from the phone. I just wanted to see his reaction – the coldness remained, but he was confused as well.

"Dude, take a hike," Gary said, slamming the door in my face.

"What a nice guy," I said. I turned away and let the screen door bang shut behind me. I walked slowly back to the 4Runner and got in. I turned the key and rolled down the window as I gazed at the house. Was it my imagination or did the curtains move slightly?

I waited and watched. It was my turn to play the intimidation card. Let him know I didn't buy his story, that I'd keep on him. My stomach growled. I'd not eaten breakfast and now it was past lunch. A burger sounded good. I was debating where to get some fast food when the front door flew open and Gary stormed out onto the lawn. "Get outta here or I'll call the cops," he hollered at me. It was most likely an empty threat as I didn't get the sense Gary would want the police around, but I figured I'd gotten under his skin enough. I smiled and waved as I put the car in gear. Gary flipped me off. I pulled out and slowly drove off down the street.

I mulled over the conversation as I headed for a bite to eat. Gary seemed genuinely surprised that Deuce's phone had his number on it. But if he was telling the truth about not talking to Deuce, then it seemed a good guess that he was lying about lending his phone to someone else, who then called Deuce. But why did he act so confused about that? Good acting to throw me off? And more questions: if Gary *didn't* call Deuce, who did? Why was Gary evasive about that? If he didn't call Deuce, why did someone *else* use his phone to call Deuce? I'd worked myself into a mystifying circle I couldn't follow anymore...

I'd wasted more than half the day and all I'd come up with was that Gary was lying. It wasn't much. And it didn't help me find Deuce.

CHAPTER SIX

I arrived at B 52s a little after three and it wasn't very crowded. Apparently, I'd missed the lunch crowd, and since the Rockies didn't play until early evening, it was early for the baseball bunch to show up. Peter Gabriel's "Sledgehammer" greeted me as I strolled through wood doors covered with stainless steel, then looked around. I spied a few young guys in shorts and polo shirts playing pool in another room. A couple sat at a table near the front window, sipping beers and watching people walk by. I moseyed up to the bar, where a tall black woman with short dreadlocks was wrestling with a keg and cursing under her breath.

"Need some help with that?" I asked.

"Hey, Reed." She stopped and straightened up. "These things can give you fits at times, but I've got it under control."

"I don't doubt that." Natalie Bowman was a regular bartender at B-52's, and since I was a regular myself, we'd gotten to know each other. Nat was working her way through school, pre-med, and she was tough and no-nonsense. I'd seen her handle a drunk or two better than the bouncers.

"Thinking through a case?" Nat knew that when I needed time to ponder something difficult, I liked to come here, drink a beer, and play some pool. She reached into a cooler and pulled out a Fat Tire, but I waved it away. "No?" she said, surprised.

"I'm working," I said as I sat down at a barstool. "So I better pass."

"Then a Coke." She grabbed a glass and filled it with ice. Then she paused, gazing at me. "You look troubled, hon. What's up?"

"Have you seen Deuce?"

"Not since last night. Why?" She filled the glass with soda and slid it across the bar to me.

"He didn't come home. No one's seen him since last night."

Nat set the beer back in the cooler, never taking her eyes off me. "And that's not like him?"

I shook my head. "Nah, he's pretty routine. If he and Ace aren't at work, they're probably home watching movies or hanging out here. And they're almost always with each other."

"Yeah, that's true, I usually see them in here together."

"Did you see them leave last night?"

"Sure," Nat said. "They were here until we closed."

I gulped some soda. "Anything seem out of the ordinary?"

Murray Head's "One Night in Bangkok" started playing. She gazed into space and her head began bopping as she thought. "Nothing that comes to mind," she finally said. "They were chatty with some other guys as they walked out and they both waved at me when they left, but they always tell me goodbye." A smile crossed her face. Nat, like most of the bartenders, loved the Goofball Brothers.

"Was there anything about the guys they were talking to? Any trouble with them?"

"No, I don't think so, but let me see if Aaron noticed

anything." Aaron was another regular bartender, a big white guy with a chest as wide as one of the kegs behind the bar. "Hold on a sec, hon." Nat sauntered through a side door and into the kitchen.

I swiveled around on the stool and watched a TV hung up in a corner. The Dodgers were playing the Diamondbacks, and the D'backs were ahead. Not good for the Rockies, who always seemed to be chasing the lead. I'm not a big baseball fan, but I like to see the home teams do well, though it seems like the Rockies never do. The TV sound was muted and I silently sang along with Murray Head. What kind of a name was that, anyway?

"Aaron said Ace and Deuce played pool with those other guys for a while, and it all seemed friendly. They all left together," Nat said over the music. She set a plate of chips and salsa in front of me. "You look hungry."

"You're a lifesaver," I said, immediately stuffing some chips in my mouth. "The burger I ate in the car wasn't enough."

"Look at this," I said between bites. I pulled out the driver's license photo of Gary that Cal had printed for me. "This picture's a little old, and he's got a shaved head now, but do you recognize this guy?"

Nat took the paper and stepped back, holding it closer to the lights above the bar. She studied it for a moment, then shook her head. "I don't think so, but unless they're in here a lot, or they do something stupid or weird, I don't usually remember who comes and goes."

She handed the paper back and I tucked it in my pocket. "It was a long shot," I said.

"Who is he?" she asked.

"Some guy who called Deuce right around the time you closed up."

"Sorry I'm not more helpful," she shrugged. "Once everyone's out the door, we're all cleaning up so we can get out of here. Give me your number and if I see Deuce, I'll call you."

I pulled out my wallet and handed her my card, then munched some more chips.

"The ace detective," she smiled as she tucked the card into her bra.

"I don't feel that way right now," I said.

"Aw, he'll turn up. Hold on." She hustled to the end of the bar to serve a couple of women who'd just come in. They were wearing purple Rockies tee shirts. The first of the baseball fans showing up.

I polished off the chips and was finishing the last of my Coke when Aaron came in from the back.

He nodded at me curtly. "Can't find Deuce, huh?"

"Yeah, he's just up and disappeared," Nat said as she rejoined us.

"Nothing unusual happened with them?" I asked Aaron.

He scrunched his lips into a frown. "Just their ordinary weirdness."

"And those guys they were playing with didn't bother them?"

"Nah, man, those guys were cool, although I think they thought they could pull one over on Ace and Deuce, because the brothers are, you know..."

"I get it," I said.

Aaron cleared his throat. "So yeah, those guys thought they saw an easy mark – bet they could beat the brothers, make a quick buck. But then Ace and Deuce beat them handily, and it put them in their place."

"Were they mad?" Nat asked.

"Nah, it was all cool." Aaron flexed his beefy arms. "They ended up playing pool for an hour or so, bought each other a round, and it was friendly."

I mulled that over. If the guys were actually pissed at Ace and Deuce, but hiding it, could one of them have gone after Deuce? But how did he get Deuce's number? I shook my head, dismissing it.

"And the last time you saw Ace and Deuce was when they were leaving with those guys?" I asked.

"Yeah, except for when Deuce came back," Aaron said.

"What?" Nat and I said at once.

"What do you mean?" Nat pounced on him. "You told me in the back that the last time you saw the brothers was when they left with the guys they were playing pool with."

Aaron shook his head. "Nah, you asked me if I saw them leave with those guys. I did. But then when I left to go home, I saw Deuce outside talking to a guy."

"Seriously?" Nat stared at Aaron. "It didn't occur to you to tell us that?"

"I am now." Aaron was a big guy, but he was shrinking as he stood in front of Nat.

"Aaron, take a look at this," I said, interrupting before the two got into a full-blown fight. I took out the picture of Gary. "Was this the guy that Deuce was talking to? It's an old picture, but the guy looks about the same. He's bald now, and he's got tattoos all up and down both arms."

Aaron glanced at the picture and shook his head. "That wasn't the guy."

"You sure?"

"Positive. That's not the same face, and the guy last night had hair and no tattoos."

"What did he look like?" Nat asked.

Aaron shrugged. "I don't know. He was kind of tall."

"Hair color? Thin? Fat? What was he wearing?" I grilled him.

"Uh, I didn't pay attention, man." He hesitated. "I think his hair was brown...maybe black, but definitely not blond."

"And?" I prodded.

"He wasn't fat, but he had a coat on so it's hard to say." Aaron held up his hands, giving me a 'how should I know' kind of look. "He was kind of ordinary."

"That's quite a description," Nat said.

"It was dark," Aaron glared at her.

"It's okay." I leaned an elbow on the bar and sighed. "If it wasn't Gary, then who was it?"

"Who's Gary?" Aaron asked.

"This guy," I said, holding up the picture before I put it back in my pocket. "He's the guy who called Deuce last night, but he's apparently not the guy who met Deuce."

"Unless Deuce met two people," Nat offered.

"Not bad." I pointed a finger at her. "That could've happened. But then it makes things even more confusing."

I turned back to Aaron. "Did you hear what Deuce and this guy were talking about?"

"I don't have any idea. I was tired and just wanted to go home."

"So the guy didn't seem like he was threatening Deuce or anything like that?"

"I don't think so," Aaron said. "Sorry, man, I didn't notice."

Nat patted my hand. "Hon, I wish we could help you more, but duty calls." She nodded at a big group that sauntered up to the bar. "I'll call you if we see him," she said as she started preparing a drink order.

"Yeah, gotta go," Aaron pushed away from the bar. "I hope you find him."

"Thanks." I tossed a few singles on the bar and left.

I thought about what Aaron said as I walked to my car.

Gary had called Deuce, but someone else met him at the bar. The question was: who was he? I shook my head.

"Where are you, Deuce?" I muttered as I started the 4Runner and drove off, contemplating my next move. Now, in addition to my conundrum with Gary, I'd confirmed that Deuce had met someone at B 52's last night, but I had no clue as to who it was. More questions, but still no answers...

CHAPTER SEVEN

"Did you find him?" Ace asked as I let myself into his place. His face was drawn and tired, and he was nervously pacing again.

"Nope," I said. I glanced from him to Willie, who was sitting on the couch, a laptop balanced on her lap. "I take it neither of you heard from him either."

"Not a thing." Willie pursed her lips into a sad twist. "I've been looking through Deuce's computer, seeing if I can find anything."

"And?" I raised an eyebrow at her.

She shook her head. "Nothing unusual on the Internet history, no unusual documents. There's not much here. Hey," she waved a hand at Ace. "Come over here."

"He mostly uses it to play games," Ace said as he sat on the arm of the couch. "Reed, I'm really worried." Willie reached over and patted his arm.

I sprawled next to her. "I know." I rubbed my hands over my face. "I haven't come up with anything."

We sat in silence for a few minutes. The front door

suddenly opened, startling us. Bob strode inside, wearing his EMT uniform.

"I thought you had to work," Ace said, surprised, and with a bit of accusation in his voice.

"I've been trying all day to get someone to cover my shift," Bob said as he perched on the corner of the coffee table. "I was on my way to work when a friend finally called and said he'd do it, so I came straight here." He looked at me, his eyes tight. "Any progress?"

I shook my head. "I tracked down who called Deuce, a guy named Gary Granderson, but he says he didn't call Deuce. So he's lying about that, or," I threw my hands up, "he's lying about something, but I don't know what. And Deuce met someone different at B 52's after he left Ace. But I have no idea who that was either."

Bob slouched forward, rested his forearms on his knees, and stared at the floor. Then he straightened up and let out a heavy sigh. "I think it's time to call the police," he said. He stared at me, waiting for my confirmation.

I hesitated as I met his gaze. Then I nodded, feeling in a way like I was admitting defeat, but knowing he was right. It was time to get the police involved, but that wouldn't prevent me from continuing my own search.

"I..." Bob paused, then he gazed at me, his face a confused mess. "I don't know how to do this. Should I call or go down to some station?"

"It'd be better to go there," I said. "They're going to have a lot of questions. And make sure you bring pictures of Deuce."

Bob's eyes watered and he quickly brushed at them. "Okay," he said hoarsely.

"Do you want me to go with you?" I asked.

"No, you've done enough." Bob stood up and pulled out his phone. "Will pictures on this be enough?"

I started to shake my head when Ace jumped up.

"I've got some," he said, darting out of the room. He returned a moment later with a couple of small, framed photos.

"Here." For some reason, he handed them to me. I suppose I was 'the man in charge'. One photo had Ace and Deuce in it, both wearing ski outfits, their faces red from the cold, snow-capped peaks behind them. The other was just Deuce. He was leaning against a pool table, a cue in his hands, a broad grin spread across his face.

"This one," I said, handing the second one to Bob. "You can see his face better."

He looked at it mutely. I told him where the closest police station was and how to get there.

"Ace, come on." Bob gestured for his brother to follow. "We'll go down there and talk to them."

"Call me if you need anything," I said, clasping his shoulder.

"Will do."

"I feel so bad for them," Willie said as we stood on the porch, watching Bob's white, Chevy truck drive away. From the passenger window, Ace stared at us, his face pale.

I let out a long sigh.

We walked up the steps to my place. "What do we do now?" she asked.

"I don't know," I said.

"Let's see what the police say," she suggested. "Give yourself a break, and maybe your subconscious will give you some ideas."

"Maybe you're right." I let us inside, glad to be home.

"Of course I am," she said, trying to lighten the mood. "I was looking through your movie collection this morning, and since you're always telling me about film noir, I thought maybe we could watch one."

I smiled. "I like the sound of that. You have one in mind?"

"Is this one good?" Willie went to the entertainment center

and held up a DVD with Dick Powell and Claire Trevor on the cover. "It says it's a Philip Marlowe mystery, and I've heard you mention him."

"Is that one good?" I said, feigning shock. "*Murder, My Sweet?* It's a classic."

"I don't know about that, but the description sounds interesting."

"You are in for a treat," I said. I took out the DVD and popped it into the player.

"I'm going to order that pizza," she called over her shoulder as she strolled into the kitchen. "Pepperoni and black olives?"

"That works for me," I said. I got the movie ready as Willie called Pizza Hut and ordered for us. Then she returned, holding two beers in one hand and a bag of chips in the other. "A snack while we wait."

I helped her get settled.

"You can't do anything more about Deuce right now," she said, putting her arm around me.

"I know. I figured he'd show up, all goofy and saying he didn't know that anyone would worry about him."

Willie leaned into me and put her head on my shoulder. "I know."

We dove into the chips as the movie started, showing Marlowe being interrogated. I'd seen *Murder, My Sweet* a few times, and each time I was struck by Dick Powell's gritty performance.

"This is a great plot," I said. "But it's complex and can be confusing. It's based on Raymond Chandler's book, *Farewell, My Lovely*."

"Why did they change the title?"

"Powell was known for light comedy and musicals, and the producers didn't want movie-goers to think the film was a musical. *Murder, My Sweet* really captures the tough dialogue that Chandler used in the book –"

"Sh," Willie chided me. "Tell me later." We leaned back on the couch and she snuggled a bit closer to me. For a moment I could hardly focus on the movie.

We lapsed into silence. I was getting into the movie, mesmerized yet again by Powell's performance, but my mind stayed on Deuce. I wondered what Willie was thinking when I noticed that her breathing had become slow and steady.

"Willie?" I whispered.

Nothing.

Great, she was bored by film noir. Oh well, I sighed. You can't have everything.

CHAPTER EIGHT

For the second day in a row, Humphrey Bogart woke me up. Willie stirred beside me, then rolled over and breathed heavily. I grabbed the phone as I slid out of bed and dashed into the hallway, quietly closing the door behind me.

"Hello?"

"Reed, did I wake you?"

"No, I was up," I lied through a yawn. My synapses weren't firing yet and I was having trouble recognizing the voice. "What time is it?"

"Seven-fifteen, and we still haven't heard anything from Deuce."

I finally placed the voice: Bob.

"Why didn't you stop by last night?" Willie and I had finished *Murder, My Sweet*, and then watched *The Maltese Falcon*, one of the best film noir ever. Willie hadn't made it through that either, so when it was over, we went to bed.

"I took Ace for some dinner after we left the station, and then back to my house for a while. I could've called, but I didn't have anything new to tell you. By the time I brought Ace back, it was too late to bother you," he said. "Besides, what could you have done last night?"

"What did the police say?" I asked.

"Not a whole lot. They took down a description and said they'd watch for him, but there isn't much they can do."

"I figured they'd say that, and unfortunately they're right."

"What do we do now?"

"I'll keep on it," I said, hating the desperation in his voice. "Something will turn up, or better yet, Deuce is going to come home."

"Okay," Bob said. "I'm coming over to check on Ace before he goes to work. I swear, he can't do anything without Deuce." He laughed, a much-needed moment of humor. "I'll let you know the minute I hear from Deuce."

I hung up and stood in the hallway for a moment, tempted to go back in the bedroom, tempted by the woman in my bed. But before I could act on that, an even more compelling idea popped into my head. I plodded down the hallway and into my home office. I wasn't much into decorating, except for this room. Floor-to-ceiling bookshelves on one wall hold a plethora of books, among them numerous rare first-edition detective novels. A DVD case is filled with my favorite film noir and detective movies, along with an Alfred Hitchcock collection. A glass display case in the corner of the room has a first edition of *A Study in Scarlet*, by Sir Arthur Conan Doyle, and I'd recently added a beautiful copy of *The High Window*, by Raymond Chandler. They're the best things in the room. I dialed Cal as I sat down at my desk.

"What do you need?" Cal's abruptness didn't surprise me; as he wasn't known for his social graces.

"Did I wake you?"

"Of course not," he snorted. "I've been up all night working on tracing this hacker who got into my client's servers. Really made a mess of things..."

"Do you have time for something else?"

"Another bit of detective work?"

"Nothing hard."

"I wasn't worried about that."

"Oh, I forgot, I never challenge you." I chuckled. "I was wondering if you could check Deuce's phone again and see if he's received any more calls."

"No problem. You looking for any specific number?"

"Uh huh. I'll lay odds that after I visited Gary, he called Deuce."

"Let's see." I heard clicking sounds and could picture Cal's fingers dancing across his keyboard. "Here we go."

"What'd you find?"

"Gary called Deuce again, at two-thirty yesterday."

"Ha!" I slapped my hand on the desk. "I was right. That's right after I left Gary's house."

"Looks like Gary left a message."

"What did he say?"

"Hold on." More taps and clicks. "I'll hold the phone up to the speaker so you can hear it."

I waited a second and then Gary's voice came through my phone, a bit distorted because it played from Cal's computer speakers and then through the phone.

"Dude, what the hell is going on?" the message began. There was a menacing tone in his voice. "I got some detective guy, says he's your friend, coming by the house and wondering where you are. It wasn't me who called you, but...what happened last night? I got to see you, man, before you talk to anyone else. We'll get things fixed, but if you think you can just weasel out of this…" A long pause ensued. "Anyway, we need to talk, so call me."

"Wow," Cal said. "Why would Deuce be friends with someone who talks to him like that?"

"I don't know that they're friends." I grabbed a pen and paper. "Let me listen to it again."

Cal played the message again and I jotted down some notes.

"I'll make a recording of it and email to you," Cal said. "Give me half an hour."

"Uh huh," I said as I contemplated what I'd written down: *It wasn't me who called you. What happened last night?*

"Gary wasn't at B52's last night and he didn't call Deuce," I said. "He was telling the truth about that."

"So who did call Deuce using Gary's phone?"

"That's what I'd like to know, although Gary could still be lying about that. Maybe he set up Deuce and he's trying to cover his tracks." I tapped my pen on the paper, thinking. "It sounded like Gary was being cautious, not wanting to say too much."

"He knows you're on to him, and he suspects that you've hacked his phone account, so it makes sense he's being careful."

"Too bad," I said. "I guess it'd be too easy for Gary to confess over the phone and tell us where Deuce is."

"Only in the movies." Cal let out a yawn that sounded like an angry lion.

"Are you planning on sleeping at all?"

"Maybe a little bit. I'm close to nailing this hacker, so I'm going to keep at it." When Cal was working, he tended to forgo sleep.

"Can you check Deuce's phone messages every couple of hours and let me know if anyone other than Bob or Ace calls him?" I asked.

"Sure, no problem. What are you going to do?"

"I'm going to pay Gary another visit," I said. "And this time, he better have some answers."

Willie was still sleeping when I got off the phone, so I dressed as quietly as I could, left her a quick note on the night-stand, then slipped out of the house.

CHAPTER NINE

It was shortly after nine when I parked across from Gary's house. Maybe you could accuse me of stereotyping, but I somehow didn't think Gary was the type to be up early. I hoped I was right.

Typical of Colorado, the weather had changed. Beautiful yesterday, but today gray clouds hung low in the sky and cold moisture clung to the air, the type that signaled snow flurries.

The street was quiet as I trotted up the walk. I paused at Gary's front door, listening. Silence. I rang the bell and waited. After a moment, I pressed the button again. Still nothing. I couldn't bring myself to believe that Gary would be gone already. I yanked open the screen and pounded on the door.

"Gary?" I called out. It was Sunday, maybe he was at church. Naaah.

I let the screen door bang shut as I stepped back and surveyed the house. The curtains were pulled closed. I stepped between some overgrown evergreen shrubs and up to the window. I cupped my hands against the glass and peered through, but I couldn't see anything.

"What the hell are you doing?"

I jumped back, my feet catching in the bushes. I lost my balance, nearly tumbling on my ass.

"Who are you?" I asked as I caught a handful of branches. I righted myself and tried to look cool. I'm sure I didn't succeed.

"I could ask you the same thing." The owner of the voice was a tall woman with long wheat-colored hair pulled into a ponytail. She stared at me with dark blue eyes surrounded by equally dark circles. Her lips formed a thin line and her hands were on her hips. Clearly annoyed.

"I'm looking for Gary," I said, brushing dead evergreen needles from my jeans.

"Obviously. But that doesn't tell me who you are."

I introduced myself and handed her a card from my wallet. "And you are?" I asked.

"Linda."

"You live around here?"

"Next door." She held up the card, then tapped it on her leg. "A private detective, huh. What do you want with Gary?" Her voice grated, like it hadn't warmed up yet.

"A friend of mine's missing and I think Gary might know something about it."

She contemplated me for a moment. "Who's your friend?"

"Deuce Smith. Ever heard of him?"

She shook her head. "What's he look like?"

I started to describe Deuce, then pulled out my phone. "Here's a picture of him." I scrolled through some photos, found one, and showed it to her.

"Nope, never seen him."

"You sure?"

The dark eyes grew darker. "Yeah, I'm sure. You wake me up on my day off, making all that racket, and you think I'm gonna give you the runaround? Last thing I need is a sleepless night."

By the looks of her, she'd had more than a few sleepless nights. She yawned and stretched, then pulled the blue scrunchie out of her hair and ran her hands through it. "I barely got any sleep, and I got a hangover, too."

"You can go back to bed now," I said as I walked back to the porch. I glanced around while Linda looked at me. "Gary doesn't seem to be around," I said, stating the obvious.

"He hasn't been home since he left after you were here yesterday."

I jerked my head toward her, surprised. "You saw me?"

"I heard you." She paused. "Well, I heard Gary yelling at you. I peeked out my window and saw him flip you off as you drove away. You really pissed him off."

"I have a way of doing that."

"You don't have to tell me."

I rolled my eyes. Everybody's a critic. "How long have you known Gary?"

"Let's see." She gnawed at her lower lip. "I moved in here right before Gary did, and that was about two years ago."

"Are you friends?"

"No, not really," she said. "Well, sometimes Gary'll have me over for a beer or two, and maybe..." she hesitated. "And, you know, maybe something to get high, but I think that's just so I'll get off his case."

"Why are you on his case?"

She let out a short, cynical laugh. "Gary can be a real asshole. You know he's got some kind of construction job, right?"

I nodded.

"Well, I think he does some jobs on the side and he and his friends will sometimes fill up the driveway with all kinds of construction crap."

"Like what?"

"You name it, it's been here," she said, waving a hand to indicate where the stuff had been. "Boards, drywall, pipes, wiring. Sometimes they keep it in his garage, other times it's been in the driveway. I've had times where I couldn't get my car into my garage, and other times I couldn't get my car *out* of the garage. Pissed me off, too, when that happens because it's made me late for work."

"That stinks," I said.

Her nostrils flared. "And if that wasn't enough, sometimes when he's got his friends over to party, they've got the music cranked, and they park their big macho trucks in the driveway..."

"Blocking you," I finished.

"Uh huh. I've gotten in his face a time or two about it, and threatened to call the cops. Then suddenly he's nice as pie, offering to have me over for a few beers, maybe a little more."

Drugs as a bribe for silence.

"Doesn't sound like he's such a great neighbor."

"No, but I've had worse."

"Has Gary ever been in trouble?"

She shrugged as she played with the scrunchie. "Not that I know of."

"Nobody called about the noise or partying?"

She jerked her head toward the street. "Nobody around here's gonna call the cops. People keep to themselves. Except when a detective comes around, banging on doors."

I held up my hands. "My timing's bad. So shoot me." Then I said, "Have you noticed anything unusual lately?"

She thought for a moment. "With Gary? No, not really."

I took in a breath and let it out slowly. She redid her pony-tail, without taking her eyes off me.

"Are you sure Gary didn't come home last night? Maybe you didn't hear him?" I finally asked.

She shook her head. "If Gary was here on a Saturday night, I'd know it."

"How so?" I asked.

"Guys are always coming and going, especially on the weekends. And they aren't quiet. There's music or the television, or arguing. This time of year, I keep my windows open." She tipped her head up toward the gray sky. "At least last night I did. My kitchen window's in the back and I can hear them in the yard, or the music coming from his house. Trust me, you can hear what goes on around here."

"Or," I hesitated for a second, "maybe you came by, looking for something to spice up the night?"

She grinned, then gave me an appreciative nod. She'd been caught. "Maybe. So sue me."

"Not worth the trouble." I stepped off the porch. "If Gary comes home, will you give me a call? I really need to talk to him."

She held up the card again, considering it. "I might."

"It's important."

She made a big deal of looking agreeable. "I'll call. You could always try to catch him at work."

"I thought of that. But that means I have to wait until tomorrow."

"I guess you can't have everything."

So true. I waved as I headed down the driveway to my car. When I glanced back, she was gone.

CHAPTER TEN

I ended up spending the day doing one of the least glamorous and most tedious of detective duties: waiting for someone to show up. I sat in my car, listening to music, waiting for Gary to come home. An hour later, Linda finally noticed I was still there. She came out with a cup of coffee.

"You could be waiting a long time," she said, holding out the cup. She'd put on some makeup, and the dark circles were gone. She was dressed in black slacks and a white blouse, and the scrunchie in her hair was now black.

The aroma made my mouth water. "I better pass," I said. "If I drink that, in an hour I'll need a bathroom."

She shrugged. "Suit yourself." She took a sip. "I'd offer to let you stay with me, but I've got to go to work."

"You think I have a long wait?" I asked.

"Yep. If Gary was out partying last night, who knows when he'll be home."

She strolled back inside and a moment later, her garage door opened. A tan, older model Honda Civic backed out. She waved at me as she drove by.

I yawned. I could've used the coffee. Minutes passed, then hours, but still no Gary. I called Willie but she didn't answer, so I left a message telling her I wasn't sure when I'd be home but that I hoped to see her today. By noon, my stomach was growling. At two, the Denver Broncos game started and I tuned in to it on the radio. I love football and it was a good game. I wished I was home watching it.

Three hours later, the game was almost over, with the Broncos ahead, when a black Dodge truck drove down the street. It slowed in front of the driveway, and before I could duck, Gary spied me sitting in the 4Runner. He hollered something at me as he flipped me the finger, gunned the engine, and the truck peeled off down the street.

"Damn," I said, starting the 4Runner. I slammed it into gear, cranked a U-turn and hit the gas.

The truck was at the corner. It turned right and disappeared. I raced to the corner and followed it. Gary was flying down Evans. The truck crossed Broadway, and the light turned yellow. I floored the gas and the 4Runner shot through the intersection. Up ahead, Gary zipped around cars. I glanced down. I was approaching sixty.

A car turned onto Evans in front of Gary's truck. He slammed on his brakes, then careened onto a side street with me right behind him. Cars lined either side of the road, leaving a narrow lane in the middle. Halfway down the block, the truck suddenly stopped and I had to hit my brakes hard, skidding to a stop inches from his bumper.

Gary flew out of the cab, shouting obscenities at me.

"I just want to talk," I shouted. I started to get out.

Gary reached into the truck bed and grabbed a short piece of wood. He stalked toward me, wielding it like a baseball bat.

"Shit," I muttered. I jerked the car into reverse and hit the gas. The 4Runner's wheels squealed as the car shot backward.

Gary's swipe at the hood of the 4Runner missed. I kept backing up with Gary running toward me. I finally found a space between two cars. I veered into it, my rear wheels jumping up on the curb. I spun the steering wheel, put the car into drive, and zoomed back toward Evans. In the rearview mirror, I saw Gary hurl the piece of wood at my car. It clattered harmlessly to the ground. Gary stood in the middle of the road, shouting at me.

So much for trying to talk to him. I drove home, thinking about Gary. He didn't know where Deuce was, and he didn't want to talk to me about it. What was he hiding? How could I get to him? An idea formed: if he didn't want to talk to me at his house, I'd try his work. I doubted he would threaten me with his coworkers and boss around.

———

When I got home, I knocked on Ace's door, but no one answered. I went upstairs and entered my empty house.

"Willie?" I called out. I glanced around and saw a note sitting on the coffee table.

Hey, handsome, sorry I missed your call. I had a great time last night. I checked on Ace before he went to work, and unfortunately, I have to go to work, too. I won't be home until late, so I'll call you tomorrow.

She signed it with just a *W*.

"Damn," I said into the silence.

Willie hated that I was a detective. She worried about me and whether I'd come home safely. She was a nurse at Denver Health, and she worked odd hours and shifts – sometimes nights and weekends – and right now, I hated *her* job. I tossed the note back on the table. So much for spending the day with her.

I fixed a sandwich and went into my office. As I ate, I looked up the address for Criss Cross Construction. It was a big company with multiple job sites both in Denver and out of state. The president was Lon Carlson. I had no way of knowing which project Gary worked at, so I figured I'd go by the main office and see if I could talk to Mr. Carlson and get the information that way. I mapped out how to get there, then called Bob.

"Still no news?" he asked.

"No," I said. "Is Ace with you?"

"Yeah, I don't want him to be alone."

"Good," I said. "Do you know where Deuce worked?"

"Yeah, Criss Cross."

"I mean which site?"

"No," he said slowly. "He was working on a bridge project, but I think that changed recently."

"Okay. I'm going to visit Deuce's work tomorrow, so if it's okay with you, I'll let them know what's going on, and talk to his boss or coworkers. Maybe they know something."

"Sure, that's fine, but couldn't you just call?"

"I'm following up on one of his coworkers, too," I said. "I'll keep you posted."

I hung up, took my plate back to the kitchen, and then went into my bedroom. I sprawled out on the bed, my face in the pillows. I smelled Willie's perfume and wished she were here. I lay morosely for a minute, then flipped over. I grabbed the remote and turned on the television. The Sunday night game was on. I closed my eyes and listened to it...and soon I dozed off.

When I awoke, it was dark outside and the game was over. And my phone was ringing.

"Reed, honey, is that you?"

"Hi, Mom, how are you?"

"Why didn't you call and tell us about Deuce?" She had a

way of launching right into something, sans any chit-chat. "Joyce Smith called us this morning, just as worried as can be. She said no one's heard from Deuce since Friday night!"

I suppose Bob Smith had had to let his mom about Deuce's disappearance. What a difficult call that must have been. Joyce Smith and my mom have known each other for years, since their country club days in Denver. Now they all live the retiree life in Florida, and she and my mom still talk almost every day. Or, more accurately, mostly my mom talks and Joyce listens. I sometimes felt sorry for her, dealing with the Brothers and my mother.

"Yes, that's true. I –" I said.

"That's just not like Deuce, is it?" she interrupted. "Joyce said that he and Ace are like two peas in a pod, and that's what I remember of them, so isn't it strange that no one knows where he is?" When my mother got going, it was hard to stop her. "You're a detective – can't you help? You know I don't approve of that business you're in, but since you refuse to get another job, put your skills to work. Have you looked around for him?"

I rolled my eyes, hoping she could hear it through the phone. "I've looked high and low."

"Don't get fresh," she sniffed, noting my tone. She had a way of sniffing to show her disdain, usually at my jokes. "You know your father and I worry about you – who knows what might happen to you – but surely you can do something."

Oh mother, if you only knew what has already happened to me in this 'business', I thought. "I really am trying to find him," I said. "I've got a lead or two; unfortunately I have to wait until tomorrow to follow up on some of it."

"Oh, that's not good, is it?"

"No, it's not."

"Well, let me know okay? Oh, how's Willie? Are you still

dating her? I'm so glad you found someone nice." When it comes to her son, my mother has three worries: that I'm doing drugs; that I'm in perpetual danger because of my job; and that I'll die alone, never having given her grandchildren.

On the first, she needn't worry, as my last illicit drug use was in college. On the second, I was tempted to tell her all about the perils my profession had put me in, but then I'd never hear the end of it. And on the third, I might have been guilty of perpetuating that fear. I hadn't had that many girlfriends since college; I was too busy flitting from job to job, trying to find something that didn't bore me. And although I think I'm okay-looking – if you ignore my dull hazel eyes – my lack of stability wasn't an attractive quality. At least now I seemed to have a girl-friend, which was progress. .

"Yes, I'm still dating Willie," I said.

"Wonderful, dear. Your father and I are excited to meet her."

"And she can't wait to meet you."

We launched into small talk for a few minutes and I deftly managed to hang up before she was able to tell me about her latest visit to the mall. Some things a son just doesn't want to know.

Willie was at work. Ace was over at Bob's. Deuce was...who knew where. I was alone. There didn't seem to be much else to do, so I undressed and crawled into bed. I was just settling in when the phone rang again.

"You still up?" Willie asked, her voice tired.

"Hey," I said. "Aren't you at work?"

"I got off early. Want some company?"

"You have no idea how much."

"Bad day? It's not Deuce, is it?"

"Still no Deuce. Come on over and I'll tell you all about it."

At least my day would end on a good note.

CHAPTER ELEVEN

The headquarters of Criss Cross Construction was a two-story brick building located in Arvada, northwest of downtown Denver. I parked in a lot across the street and went in the building. Inside was a cavernous foyer with a model of a power plant placed in the middle and huge fake trees on either side. Off to the left was a winding staircase with a wrought-iron railing. I took the steps two-at-a-time up to the second floor. A gray-haired woman sat at a computer behind a long mahogany desk. On the wall behind her was a large wooden sign: three C's intertwined, with the company name to the right. She paused when she saw me.

"May I help you?" She had a low, sultry voice, like some of the femme fatales in the movies I loved.

I put on my best smile. "I hope so. You have an employee that works for you named Gary Granderson."

"Gary Granderson?"

"Yes, and Deuce Smith."

"Deuce...Smith?" The words came out like they were sour on her tongue.

"Yes. I'm wondering if you could tell me what construction sites they work at."

Her lips formed into a thin line. "I'm afraid that's impossible. I can't give out information about employees."

"It's very important."

"As I said, I can't give out that information."

I figured it would go this way, so it was time to try another tact. "Then I'd like to speak to Lon Carlson," I said.

She surveyed me more closely. "Mr. Carlson is a very busy man, and he doesn't have time for interruptions. What is this regarding?"

"It's a private matter."

"Then I'm afraid you'll have to come back." She glanced at her monitor and tapped her keyboard. "I'll see when Mr. Carlson is available later this week."

"I need to speak to him now," I said.

She paused, then sat just a bit straighter. "What is this regarding?" she repeated. She had a very busy boss, and it was her job to keep things running smoothly for him. Interruptions like me were not tolerated. Or so she thought.

"That's between me and Mr. Carlson." I pulled out a business card and handed it to her.

She hesitated, as if I were handing her a snot-filled Kleenex, then took the card by the edge. She read the card and her eyes darted up to me and back to the card.

"Is there some sort of trouble?"

"It's private," I repeated, staring her down.

"I'll see if he can make time for you," she said, picking up the phone. By her tone, I could tell that she expected the answer to be a negative. She waited a moment, then spoke expertly into the receiver, so discreetly I only made out a word or two. She listened and her eyebrows arched in surprise.

"All right, sir." She hung up the phone and stood up,

straightening her skirt. "He can give you five minutes before he has a meeting."

"Thank you." I tried to hide the smirk on my face.

I followed her down a short hallway, past multiple cubicles where Criss Cross employees were hard at work. She stopped at the end of the hall and stood by an open door to a corner office.

"Mr. Ferguson," she announced.

"How can I help you?" said Carlson. He was a big man, build like a linebacker, with a few extra pounds around the waist. His blue tie was knotted neatly, but the top button of his pressed white shirt was undone and his sleeves were rolled up. A man who'd already put in a hard day's work by nine a.m. He stepped around a desk twice the size of his secretary's and offered me a meaty hand. "Lon Carlson."

His handshake was forceful.

"Would you like something to drink? Coffee? Water?"

"I'm fine, thanks," I said.

He nodded at the gray-haired woman. "Thank you, Edna," he said. She gave me one final, cursory glance and shut the door.

"Thanks for seeing me," I said.

"Getting a visit from a private investigator certainly piques my interest. Please, sit." He waved at a leather chair across from his desk.

I sat down and waited as he settled himself behind his desk.

He contemplated me for a moment. "What's this about?"

"You have an employee named Deuce Smith who works for you," I began.

"That name's not familiar." His brow wrinkled. "Is he a laborer at one of the job sites?"

"Yes."

"I'm sorry, but I don't, uh...Deuce, did you say?" He took a sip from a black mug that said 'Boss' on it.

I nodded.

"I don't know him. We've got a lot of jobs going and it's impossible for me to know everyone who works for me personally."

"I understand."

"Is Deuce is some kind of trouble?"

"I think so. He hasn't been seen since Friday night."

Carlson leaned forward and put his elbows on the desk. His arms stretched the material of his shirt.

"That *is* concerning," he said. "What do you think happened to him?"

"I wish I knew."

"How can I help?"

"Can you tell me what job site he worked at? I'd like to talk to his coworkers and maybe his supervisor, see if they noticed anything unusual."

"Sure, I'll have Edna look that up." He picked up the phone and hit a button.

I held up a hand. "And can you confirm that Gary Granderson works at the same site?"

"Edna, I need you to look up a couple of employees. Deuce?" he raised his eyebrows at me.

"Smith," I said.

"Smith," he repeated into the phone. "And Gary Granderson. Let me know what sites they're working at." He sat back and eyed me. "Deuce. That's an unusual name."

I shrugged. A long silence ensued, in which Carlson stared at me and I stared out the window at the maple trees in a small park across the street. The sun shone brightly and the maple leaves were a brilliant red color. I found myself relieved that I didn't have a desk job; my paychecks may not be regular, but being a private investigator suits my rather extroverted personality.

Carlson's phone buzzed. He picked it up and listened for a second. "Okay, thanks." He hung up and looked at me. "They both work at the Vanguard project. It's that new high-rise downtown. It's off of 15th and California, near the convention center."

"I can find it," I said.

"It's quite a project. Thirty stories, with condos and office space. It'll have underground parking, and space for restaurants. The condos will be luxury two and three bedrooms."

I already knew that from my research, but I let him blow his horn. "Sounds interesting," I said when he took a breath. "Who's Deuce's boss at the site?"

"Chuck Fitzhugh is the project manager."

"Will he be able to talk to me?"

"I'll call him and let him know you're coming out." Carlson stood up, indicating the meeting was over. "He's pretty busy but I'll tell him to make a few minutes for you. There's an office trailer right near the street; you can't miss it. Look for him there."

I stood up, too. "Thank you."

"I just hope that Deuce turns up," he said as he showed me out of his office.

"I do, too," I said.

I walked down the hallway and as I passed Edna, she gave me a disdainful look. I'm sure she was unhappy that I had bothered her boss. Or maybe she was jealous because she didn't know what our conversation was about.

"You've been as helpful as Phyllis Dietrichson," I said to Edna as I passed, referring to the duplicitous femme fatale in *Double Indemnity*.

Let her spin with that.

I smiled as I trotted down the stairs and outside.

CHAPTER TWELVE

The Vanguard project was located near the Colorado Convention Center on the southern edge of downtown. The office trailer was right where Lon Carlson said it would be. I drove through the gate and parked in front of the trailer, next to a full-sized Chevy truck. The rumbling of heavy machinery filled the air as I walked up wooden stairs to the trailer door and let myself in.

The trailer was decorated in a lovely dark wood paneling that had gone out of style in the '70s. The linoleum on the floor was dirty and worn – too many work boots on it. Cheap blinds covered the windows, and framed posters, the kind with nature pictures and slogans meant to inspire – *Quality Will Always Shine Through* – hung on the walls. Right next to the door was a beat-up metal desk. The woman behind it looked up when I entered. She had on black slacks and a green blouse that matched her eyes.

"Can I help you?" Already she was more pleasant than Edna. Maybe it was the smile on her face.

I introduced myself and before I could say more she said,

"Oh yes, Chuck said you'd be by. They're pouring a section of concrete today, but he said if you didn't mind the chaos, you could talk to him out there."

"Suits me fine."

"Great. You'll have to wear this." She pushed back from the desk, grabbed an old white hardhat from a box on the floor behind her, and stood up.

I took the hardhat from her. "How do I look?" I asked, tipping the hat like it was a fedora.

She grinned. "It's not about the look." She pointed to a yellow sign with black letters by the door: *Safety First*.

"Ah." I crammed the hardhat down on my head.

"Let me show you where he is," she said.

I followed her outside.

"We've got a lot of trucks coming in today," she hollered over her shoulder as we waited while a cement truck rumbled by. I waved away the sudden cloud of dust around us.

We crossed a dirt lot and walked onto the building site. The structure was in the initial stages, with the concrete and steel columns and beams rising up a few stories. A large trailer truck, loaded with rebar, was parked nearby. A light breeze stirred, carrying with it a smell of diesel and damp dirt. Metal rang against metal, saws buzzed, and construction workers milled about.

We turned a corner. Up ahead, the cement truck was backed up to an area that had been excavated and had rebar spread all across it. Obviously the floor for this part of the building.

"Chuck's over there, in the gray shirt." She pointed to a man in worn jeans, gray Polo shirt, heavy work boots, and hardhat who stood near the cement truck.

"Thanks," I said. I walked past a stack of long pipes and as I approached Chuck Fitzhugh, he turned and saw me.

"You must be Reed Ferguson," he said. He was tall and thin, with disproportionately wide shoulders and long arms.

"Thanks for taking the time to speak with me," I said, elevating my voice above the din.

"No problem. Sorry we have to talk out here. The office would be better, but I've got to oversee this." He gestured at the commotion around us. "They had a problem when they poured the last area, so I need to make sure things go better this time around."

"You've got a lot going on here."

Fitzhugh nodded. "I wondered why Deuce was so late, and then I get a call from Mr. Carlson, saying that Deuce wouldn't be coming in to work, and that a private investigator wants to talk to me." He stepped back and eyed me. "What's going on?"

"No one's seen Deuce since Friday night. He's not the type to disappear for the entire weekend, and he definitely isn't the type to blow off work."

Worry lines creased Fitzhugh's tanned face. "That's true. Deuce has been working on this project for almost a year and he hasn't missed a day."

"Did you see him last Friday?"

"Yeah, but not for very long. Hey, watch that part over there," Fitzhugh shouted at a guy over by the corner section. Then he turned back to me. "There's a lunch wagon that comes on site and Deuce was waiting in line to get something. I talked to him while we waited."

"Did he act unusual, or say anything that sticks out?"

Fitzhugh thought for a second while we watched concrete pour out of the sluice. "No, not really. Wait, he did say something about guns, that he needed to learn how to shoot, or he was going to go shoot guns, something like that."

I laughed. "He went with me to the firing range Friday night."

"That must've been it then. Hold on."

A muscular guy with spiky black hair walked over. He gave me a onceover, then turned to Fitzhugh. "What about that other section?" he asked in a deep voice.

Fitzhugh spoke to him for a second. "Hold on," he said to me and then they moved off. While I waited, I watched a guy wearing black rubber boots work with a hose attached to a small machine. "Sorry about that," he said when he returned.

"What's that guy doing?" I asked, gesturing at the guy with the hose.

"That's called a vibrator," he said. I resisted the juvenile urge to laugh. He pointed at the sluice. "When the cement is poured, air pockets can form. You use the vibrator to get rid of them. If you don't, it can hurt the structural integrity."

I nodded. The things I learn. "So, did Deuce get along with his coworkers?"

"Yeah, no problems there. He's a pretty popular guy. Kind of simple, but he works hard and doesn't make mistakes, and the guys respect that. Hell, so do I."

"You didn't see him after lunch?"

"No." Fitzhugh stayed focused on the cement being poured. "I can ask around, see if any of his coworkers noticed anything, or if he said anything unusual to them."

"Sure," I said, giving him a business card, although I didn't expect much from that.

"I don't know what else to tell you," he said. "If you don't need anything else..."

"Just one more thing." I had a habit of sounding like Peter Falks' Columbo. "There's a guy named Gary Granderson who also works for you."

"Uh huh. He started working for me on the project before this one." Fitzhugh frowned. "Talk about two different guys."

"What do you mean?"

"Deuce is pretty laid back, a nice guy. Gary, on the other hand…" He tipped his head back and forth, mulling over what to say. I waited him out. "Let's just say Gary isn't such a nice guy."

"Problems with his coworkers?" I asked.

"Not necessarily problems." He hesitated. "It's just that he always seems to have a chip on his shoulder, complaining about things around here. Don't get me wrong, he gets the job done, but I don't think the guys like him much."

"He's a bit of a hothead," I agreed.

He nodded.

"Did Gary actually work with Deuce here?"

"Yeah, Gary oversaw some of Deuce's construction."

"Interesting," I said. Gary seemed to be full of lies.

Fitzhugh turned to me. "What?"

"I talked with Gary over the weekend and he said he hardly knew Deuce."

"No, they work here together."

"What else can you tell me about Gary?" I asked.

"You think he's mixed up in Deuce's disappearance?"

"That's what I'd like to know. He talked to Deuce last Friday night."

"It's a little surprising that Deuce would hang around with Gary." He gave a little shrug. "They don't seem anything alike. But I guess that's their business."

"So, no trouble between Deuce and Gary?"

"Not that I've heard or seen."

"Is Gary reliable?"

"Yeah," he nodded. "Well, except for today." He opened his mouth, then stopped.

"What?"

"Gary didn't show up today, either."

"He called in sick?"

Fitzhugh shook his head. "No, he just didn't show. A couple of the guys who have his number said they tried to call him, but he didn't answer."

I drew in a breath and let it out slowly. A gnawing started in my stomach.

"You think something's happened to Gary, too?" he asked, the worry lines back.

"I don't know," I said. I shook his hand. "You've got my card. If you think of anything else, even if it doesn't seem important, give me a call."

"Absolutely." He closed his eyes for a second, looking tired. "Keep me posted, okay? I'd hate to see anything bad happen to either of them."

"I will," I said.

I walked back to the office and turned in my hardhat. The office lady smiled at me again, and wished me a nice day, but somehow I thought it wasn't going to be so.

CHAPTER THIRTEEN

It seemed Gary hadn't told me the truth about anything. It was time to pay him another visit, and this time, I wasn't going to let him lie to me. If he was there. The knot in my stomach grew as I drove south from downtown to Gary's house.

I parked across the street from the duplex and got out. It looked the same as yesterday, with the curtains drawn and the front door closed. No way to tell if anyone was home. As I walked up the driveway, Linda came out of her place in jeans and a yellow blouse, and her hair was down.

"Hey, it's the detective," she said. Did I detect a mocking tone? "Still haven't talked to Gary?"

I shook my head. "Have you seen him?"

"Nope. He was around last night, though. Another of his buddies parked his big old truck in the driveway. I banged on the door to get them to move it, but no one answered." She gestured at her Honda, parked at the curb. "I had to park there."

"Why wouldn't Gary answer the door?" I asked.

She shrugged. "I don't know. He doesn't have a reason to

avoid me. Just because I want to keep my car in the garage. Whatever..."

"You sure he was at home?"

She seemed taken aback. "What do you mean?"

"You didn't see Gary, but did you hear him? Or his friends?"

"I didn't see anyone at the time." She twisted a finger through her hair as she thought. "I just figured they were there because the truck was in the driveway. But later someone left."

"Did you see him?"

"Sort of. He was kind of tall." I waited for more. "It was dark," she finally said. She fixed a hard gaze at me. "What's going on?"

"Gary didn't show up for work this morning," I said. I pointed to his door. "So is he here now, or did he leave with someone in the truck last night?"

"He didn't leave with the other guy." She leaned closer to me and I got a whiff of perfume and stale cigarettes. "You think something's happened to him?"

"I don't know," I said. "Tell me about the truck."

"It was just a truck."

"Color?"

"Blue. Wait, maybe it was black." She must not have liked the look on my face because she threw up her palms and repeated, "It was dark!"

"It's okay," I said, trying to ease her defensiveness. "It probably doesn't matter. Was there anything else about the truck? Dents in it or oversized tires? Full-sized cab?"

She gazed at the driveway, as if picturing the truck. "There was something on the doors, like a company logo."

"What did it say?"

"I don't know." Almost a whine. "Do you know how many trucks have parked here with logos on them? Gary's buddies are all in construction. There's electrical trucks, plumbing, and stuff."

"You can't remember anything about it?" I prodded.

A pause. "I think it had circles on it," she said.

"Circles?"

"Yeah." She took her index finger and made round motions in the air.

"That's a...good description," I said. "Do you know how long it was parked here?"

"Beats me. It wasn't there when I left...well," she exhaled, "You know that. And the truck was here when I got home."

"Where do you work?"

"I bartend at Smoky Joe's. It's a bar near Mile High." She referenced Sports Authority Field at Mile High, where the Broncos play. Most people just call it 'Mile High'. "Game days are great, good tips, but long days."

"Anything else?"

She glanced at Gary's front door, then exhaled. "Sorry."

I nodded. "Like I said, it's probably nothing." Although I didn't feel that way at all.

She shifted from foot to foot. "Hey, I hope you find Gary, but I was just on my way out. I gotta go." With that, she sauntered past me to her car.

"Thanks for the circle tip," I said to no one. "What the hell do I do with that?"

I went up to Gary's door and knocked. Silence. I knocked again, harder, then glanced at my watch. Ten-thirty.

I stepped off the porch and looked up and down the street: not a soul in sight. Most people were at work, and the street was quiet. I turned back to the house. *What would Bogie do?*

"Check the back," I whispered as I headed around the side of the house.

A weathered wood fence and gate greeted me. I wasted no

time in letting myself into the back yard. I closed the gate and walked slowly along the side of the house to the end. I peered around the corner of the house. The yard was postcard-sized, with brown grass in desperate need of mowing. A small covered porch had piles of wiring, copper pipes, and rebar strewn about. Did Gary have his own construction business on the side? I made a mental note to check.

I made my way through the mess to the back door. There was no screen, just a heavy wood door in need of paint. I knocked again, not expecting anything. I tried the knob. It turned. I eased the door open. "Gary?"

Nothing. Just a greeting of stale heat.

I took a deep breath, trying to ease the tension buzzing through me. If Gary was inside, sleeping off a hangover, I didn't relish running into him. I'd bet he had more than a piece of wood inside. Like a bat...or a gun.

I stepped into a tiny kitchen. There was just enough room for a refrigerator, stove, and a table for two in the corner. A microwave sat on a counter next to a sink full of empty beer bottles. In two steps I crossed the kitchen and looked into the living room.

The curtains were closed tight and the room had a gloomy cast to it. A cheap entertainment center stood against one wall with a large flat-screen television and stereo system on it. A couch sat against the opposite wall. In between, next to a cluttered coffee table, Gary lay on his back on the floor, sightless eyes staring at the ceiling. It didn't take a detective to know he was dead.

CHAPTER FOURTEEN

I sucked in a breath as I fell back against the wall. My eyes locked onto Gary's face and I stared for a long moment. Gary's mouth was open as if he were surprised. I realized I'd been holding my breath so I slowly exhaled, trying to calm my suddenly churning stomach. The heat in the room felt stifling. Unlike my detective heroes, I'd never seen a dead body before.

As I blinked hard and focused, my investigative skills kicked into gear. First thought: don't disturb anything. Second thought: check the body for a pulse. I looked into the cold, dry eyes. That probably wasn't necessary. Third: call the police. I hesitated. Bogie wouldn't call the cops just yet, and neither would I.

I stepped gingerly across the carpet and bent down over the body. An acrid smell hit my nostrils. I gulped and started breathing out of my mouth.

Gary had been shot in the chest, and the front of his tee shirt was soaked in blood. The fingers of his left hand looked as if they were clawing at the bullet hole. Dried blood covered the fingernails and a small pool of blood had oozed out beneath him. He had been lying there for a number of hours.

I studied the bullet wound closely. I wasn't a forensics expert, but I thought I spied some dark residue on the shirt around the bullet hole. That indicated Gary had been shot at very close range. Suicide? But where was the gun?

I stood up straight and looked around. Gary's right hand was splayed out from his body, the hand empty, and there was no gun anywhere around him. If he'd killed himself, he'd be the first person to successfully hide the gun used to commit the act. No question this was murder.

I backed up and let my eyes rove around the room, taking everything in. The coffee table was askew, not parallel with the couch as it would normally be, as if Gary and his killer scuffled before Gary was shot. A beer bottle was tipped over on the floor, its contents soaking into the carpet.

The television was on, showing some morning cable sports show I didn't recognize. The hosts looked to be debating, pointing at each other, but the sound was off. I looked around for remotes and saw a couple on the floor near the couch. Had the killer turned off the sound before he left, or had Gary when he let the killer in?

A reclining chair in the corner and a bookcase filled with DVDs comprised the rest of the furniture. The walls were bare except for a poster of a skier flying off a cliff, pristine white powder below him.

I tried to reconstruct what might've happened. One scenario was that Gary got into an argument with one of his buddies, the buddy pulls a gun and shoots Gary. But if they were partying, wouldn't Linda have heard them? So maybe Gary was alone and someone came calling.

Second scenario: Gary's watching TV when someone rings the bell. He opens the door and lets the person into the living room. Did the killer already have his gun out? If so, he wouldn't want anyone to see him, so he would force Gary to move away from the door. Since Gary lay in the middle of the room, it stood to reason that either this happened or Gary talked with the killer for a least a moment or two before a gun was drawn. But I had no way of knowing. Did Gary try to reason with the killer? And then they argued and then the killer shot him?

"I have no idea and you can't tell me," I murmured as I glanced back at Gary.

Once the killer struck, what did he do? I strode over to the front door, careful not to disturb anything. The door was shut, but on close examination, I saw that the deadbolt was not locked. Easy for the killer to let himself out but keep others from getting in. Unless the killer left by the back door.

Too many questions, and not enough answers.

I went down the hallway where there was a tiny bathroom and a bedroom. I poked my head in the bathroom and flicked on the light with my phone so I wouldn't leave any prints. Like the rest of the house, it was in need of a good cleaning. Toothpaste residue in the sink, water spots on the mirror, grime in the tub. But nothing stood out.

Same with the bedroom. A double bed with rumpled sheets, bare walls, and dirty clothes on the floor. The closet door was open. I glanced inside. Jeans and a few shirts hanging up, more dirty clothes in a pile. On a dresser near the door I saw some spare change, papers and a notepad. I looked at the pad. A list of some company names and another list of websites were scrawled on it.

As I studied it I became aware of noise from outside. A vehicle was nearing the house, and the rumble told me it was a truck. I stood still and listened. The engine growl grew louder as the vehicle pulled into the drive. Then the engine died. Without thinking, I tore the paper off the pad and stuffed it in my pocket. I tiptoed out of the room and down the hall, freezing as the clang of the doorbell pierced the silence.

I peeked around the corner, half expecting the door to open. The bell rang again and then I jumped as the person pounded on the door.

"Hey, man, open up," a muffled male voice said from outside.

I waited, the silence deafening. How long would it take him to leave? Sweat dripped off my face.

"Gary, you in there?"

The clear, suddenly un-muted voice startled me. Gary's visitor had come to the big front casement window. I hadn't noticed that one side was cranked open, and the man was calling through the screen. He shuffled on his feet and then his shadow appeared in the middle of the window, where the curtains came together. He was trying to see inside. After a moment, he moved back to the open window.

"Hey man, where the hell are you? We gotta dump this stuff." A heavy sigh and a curse. "How am I supposed to load the stuff from the back?"

My eyes darted past Gary's body and toward the kitchen. What if he came around and tried the back door as I'd done? I was a sitting duck. My mind raced. Should I let myself out the back door and into the alley? Would he hear me if I did?

Rustling sounds came from the window and then, "Hey, it's me."

He was talking to someone on his cell.

"He ain't home." Short pause. "I don't know. I knocked on the door and called through the window. You want me to get the stuff out back?"

I took a couple of quiet steps into the room.

"All right. I'll be back soon."

The man moved away from the window. I took another few steps, trying to see where he'd gone. Then a car door slammed and the truck roared to life. I dashed to the window and carefully pulled the curtain aside. Through the crack I saw a forest-green diesel truck back out of the driveway. The driver was a young man with shoulder-length hair and a goatee. Once on the street, he gunned the engine and peeled away, tires screeching, rubber smoke trailing behind. I focused on the license plate, repeating it to myself until I memorized it.

Breathing a sigh of relief, I let the curtain fall back into place. I had no idea who that was, and I was relieved I didn't have to explain to him why I was there. I was finished looking around, but I thought about my next move. Should I leave, then call the police anonymously? That's probably what the old detectives would do. But then how would I explain my prints on the back door knob, and the fibers and hair I'm sure I'd left around the body, and maybe throughout the house? It would be better to admit I came in and found the body, and then called the police.

Decision made, I let myself out the back door and went around the house to my car. I got in, called the police, and reported the body. Then I sat back to wait.

CHAPTER FIFTEEN

I turned on the radio, listening to *The Queen Is Dead* by The Smiths. The queen may not be dead, but Gary sure was. It was a long song, and it was almost finished when a cop car drove down the block and parked in front of the duplex. A moment later a blue '65 Ford Mustang parked behind it, followed by a brown sedan. A uniformed cop emerged from the police car, and he waited as a tall blond got out of the Mustang and two men got out of the sedan. The detectives.

I hurried across the street.

"Hey, hold up." One of the guys turned, frowning and glaring at me. He wore a brown suit with a white shirt, and he hitched his pants up over a large gut.

"I called you," I said, my hands up.

"Oh yeah?" he growled at me, flashing yellow-stained teeth.

The woman surveyed me for a few seconds, so I, in turn, assessed her. She was quite attractive, in her tan slacks and light blue blouse, a Denver P.D. shield attached to her belt. Not at all the stereotype of a butch female cop. A quick thought hit me: what was she thinking of *me*?

The uniform approached. "Front door's locked. No one answers."

She cocked an eyebrow at me.

"I went through the back door," I explained.

"Stay with him," she ordered the uniform. "Get a statement." With a nod of her head, the other two suits followed her through the gate.

"What's your name, bud," the uniform said, a little more gruffly than was necessary.

I was sorely tempted to say "Philip Marlowe", the detective in *The Big Sleep*. But I knew I'd be caught, and if the uniform happened to know the name, somehow I didn't think he'd be amused. So I rattled off my name, address and then gave him a quick rundown of why I was there. I was certain it wouldn't be the first time I'd be explaining my presence there. I took a card from my wallet and explained that I was a private investigator, but he wasn't impressed. He grabbed the card, blinked at it, and tucked it into his notepad.

"Over here," he said, jerking a thumb at his car.

We walked over and he opened the back door. "You can wait here."

I sat on the edge of the seat but left the door open. The sun was warm on me as I propped an arm on the door and watched the house. The uniform stood on the sidewalk, talking into his radio, checking on me. He made a few notes, then signed off. Then we waited. A few minutes later, more cars rolled up. People with bags and cameras made their way around the house to the backyard. Crime scene technicians, and one with a black bag who I assumed was the coroner.

My phone rang. It was Willie. I started to answer, but the cop frowned at me so I shut it off. Maybe now wasn't the time to chit-chat with my girlfriend, although I hated to miss the call. But then again, she'd want to know what I was doing.

Sitting in a cop car, waiting while some detectives check on the dead body I just found. That would go over *really* well, especially since Willie's major objection to dating me was that my job was too dangerous. Her father had been a cop, and she'd shared with me worrying whether he'd come home after work each day made for a horrible childhood. She didn't want to live that way as an adult. Yeah, maybe it was better to miss the call...

I was beginning to think no one wanted to talk to me when the blond emerged from the front door. She gestured at us, so the uniform and I walked up to the porch.

"His name is Reed Ferguson," the uniform said. "He's a private dick." I wasn't sure if there was a little extra emphasis on the last word. He quickly repeated what I'd said to him, acting as if I wasn't there.

She nodded when he finished and he stepped away. The brown suit came out, leaned against the wall, took out a notepad and pen, and stared at us.

"I'm Detective Spillman," she said. Cold, coffee-colored eyes bore through me. She nodded at the suit. "That's Detective Moore."

I looked at him and he grunted.

"You're a private detective?" Spillman asked.

"Yes."

"Never heard of you," Moore grunted.

"I haven't been around long," I said.

"You called this in," Spillman said, taking control.

She was so no-nonsense that I avoided any flip comment. "Yes," was all I said.

"You know the deceased?"

"His name is...was...Gary Granderson. But I don't really know him."

"What were you doing here?"

"I came by to talk to Gary, but he didn't answer the door. I thought maybe he was trying to avoid me, so when he didn't answer, I went around back. The door was unlocked. I let myself in, and I found the body."

Succinct, to the point. How could she find any issues with that? Moore took notes while we talked.

"You just let yourself in," she repeated.

I nodded. Apparently she did have issues with my story. I needed to tread carefully.

"Through the back door?"

Another nod.

"And you found the body."

"Yes."

"And you left everything alone, came back outside and called us?"

I tried for nonchalance, like *how could I be lying to you?* "That's right." There was no way I could tell her about the guy who came to the door while I was inside, or they'd find out I was in the house longer than it takes to verify a man is dead.

"You didn't touch anything?"

I thought about the paper in my pocket. "I checked to make sure he was dead," I said, meeting her gaze. "Then I called the police."

She tipped her head up and down, just once. "Uh-huh. So if we find your hair or clothing fibers from your clothes on the body, your checking to make sure he was dead would explain it."

"I would assume so."

A bright flash briefly illuminated the doorway. They were taking pictures of the crime scene.

"What's a private detective, who knows the deceased by name, but doesn't really know him, doing here?"

"A friend of mine is missing. Gary works with my friend, but he lied to me about it. When I found out he lied, I came back to talk to him."

"And you found the body."

"No, I came back yesterday to talk to him again, but he wasn't at home. This morning I went to their work site, and I found out Gary didn't show up and no one had heard from him. That's when I came here and found him."

"Have you reported your friend missing?"

"Yes."

Spillman leaned inside. "Spats."

The other suit materialized. He was flashier than Moore, dressed in sleek black pants, a silk shirt with cufflinks, and polished wing-tipped shoes.

Spillman turned to me. "What's your friend's name?"

"Deuce Smith."

She paused for a second. She had to be wondering if I was making up the name. "Check on the report," she finally said.

He disappeared inside.

"Spats?" I said, eyebrows arched.

"Detective Youngfield," she said to me.

"Nice nickname," I murmured.

She ignored that and continued questioning me.

"You said Gary might be avoiding you."

"I thought he might be," I said.

"Why?"

"I first came by on Saturday to talk to him, he wasn't very pleasant."

"You think he's hiding something from you, or he has information about your friend?"

"The thought crossed my mind."

Spats stuck his head through the doorway. "There's a missing-persons report for a Deuce Smith, reported by his older brother."

Spillman tipped her head again, the single nod.

"So you're trying to find your friend, you think Gary has something to do with it, and you've been around here before."

"Yes." I suddenly was unsure of myself. I did a quick mental review of our conversation and I didn't like where this was headed. I glanced at Moore. He stared back, his face a blank slate.

"Or do you think Gary did something to your friend, so you came here, killed Gary, and then reported it to us?" Spillman said.

"If that's true, why would I report it?"

"To throw us off track."

Our eyes locked. I waited her out. She was forced to look away when Spats came back out.

"We'll need his prints, Spillman," he said, pronouncing it 'Speelmahn'.

"No problem," I said, but I was getting nervous. What happened if and when they found out I searched around the house?

He turned to me. "You just touched the doorknob and nothing else?"

I nodded.

"Okay, let's get this done." He went inside and returned with an inkpad and fingerprint card. He was careful as he printed me, not wanting to get ink on himself. When he completed the job, he handed me a tissue. I worked on my hand, but the ink remained.

"Am I a suspect?" I asked.

"Until we can eliminate you."

Great. Maybe I shouldn't have called the police.

"Where were you last night?" Spillman asked.

"With my girlfriend. She came over about eleven and I was with her all night, until I left for work this morning."

Spillman nodded. "We'll need to verify that."

I rattled off Willie's number. Moore wrote it down, then poked his head inside, presumably giving the number to Spats. So much for keeping Willie in the dark. I sighed.

"Spillman," Spats called to her.

"Wait here," she ordered me, then marched inside.

I waited, my eyes on Moore. He made a few notes and then looked in the house. My phone rang again. Moore glared at me as I shut it off. It was Willie again. I was going to have a lot of explaining to do. A few minutes later, Spillman returned.

"Detective Spillman," I said, spreading my hands. "I'm trying to find my friend. What I've told you is the truth."

Spillman contemplated me for a moment. "I believe you," she said, softening just a bit. "So far your story checks out."

"Good."

"What else can you tell us?" she asked.

I shrugged. "Not much." I explained what I knew, leaving out how Cal had gotten the cell phone information.

"But you don't know how, or if, Gary's death is connected to your friend?"

"Not yet. But I'll figure it out."

"I'd appreciate it if you'd share what you find out with us, and you don't interfere with our investigation."

"Of course," I said. "Do you need me here anymore?"

Spillman shook her head. "No, but we might call you back."

I turned to go, then stopped. "Does the exchange of information go both ways?"

"No way," she snapped, then paused. "It depends on what mood I'm in."

"Thanks." I backed up. "Do you have a first name?"

She looked me up and down. "It's Sarah," she finally said.

"Nice name." I tipped a make-believe fedora at her, Bogie-style. Then I stepped off the porch and walked to my car.

She stayed on the porch, watching as I drove away.

CHAPTER SIXTEEN

I pulled over a few blocks away and sat for a moment, gathering my thoughts. I hadn't been interrogated like that, ever. Even my mother's nosiness paled in comparison. I breathed deeply for a moment and assessed the situation. Deuce was still missing. Gary was now dead. I'd found him. I'd stolen something from his house. I'd lied to the police about that. I hadn't told them about the man looking for Gary. If Spillman figured all that out, it was going to be bad for me. And if I was going to find out what happened to Deuce, and to Gary, I would have to work fast and stay ahead of her.

But first things first. I grabbed my cell phone and called Willie.

"Reed, what in the world is going *on*? I get a call from the police asking if we were together last night, and I haven't heard a word from you."

"What happened to 'Hey handsome'?"

"That's not funny. I've been worried sick."

"I know. I'm sorry." I exhaled slowly. "Remember Gary, who worked with Deuce? He's dead."

Willie gasped. "What happened? Are you all right?"

"I'm fine." I launched into a quick account of everything that happened since I'd last seen her.

"Reed, how is Deuce involved?"

"I don't know," I said. "But Gary seems to be at the center of all this."

"He did lie to you about not knowing or talking to Deuce. But now that Gary's dead, how do you find out why?"

"I don't know," I repeated, with more certainty than I actually felt. "And something he did to somebody was enough to get him killed. My play now is to figure out who killed Gary, and hopefully it'll lead me to Deuce."

"You don't think that maybe..." her voice cracked. "Do you think someone would've, you know?"

"No, I'm sure Deuce is okay," I said. "If he's involved in whatever's going on, he's probably hiding out somewhere. I could see him not knowing what to do, so he runs away instead of facing us."

"You think so?"

"Yeah, it'll be okay. Hey, I've got a couple of things to follow up on. Do you have time to check on Ace?"

"Sure, I'm off today so I'll pop over and see how he's doing." She paused. "Will I see you today?"

"I hope so."

"Okay, call me later."

"Will do."

I hung up and tossed the phone on the seat, frustrated. I wanted to go home and spend the afternoon with Willie. Instead, not only did I still need to find Deuce, I now needed to find a killer. And even though I'd tried to downplay my worry to Willie, I was scared that Deuce might've been killed, too.

I dug the piece of paper from Gary's room out of my pocket and studied it. There was a list of websites: Craigslist, Digger slist, eBay, Builder2Builder, and others. Craigslist and eBay I knew. Some of the others I didn't. Below that was another short list of construction and electrical companies.

I picked up my phone, connected to the internet, typed in Diggerslist, and a moment later the page loaded. It was billed as a home improvement classifieds site. I clicked on the *about* page, and read more. Diggerslist was similar to Craigslist, another hugely popular online classified site. But unlike Craigslist, where you could buy and sell stuff, place personal and want ads, advertise jobs, and much more, Diggerslist focused solely on buying and selling products specifically related to home improvement and construction. You could also narrow your search to where you lived. I clicked around the site for a bit, noting that it had a ton of stuff for sale, from building materials to heavy equipment, tools, interior décor and furniture.

I typed in the other site, Builder2Builder, and saw that it was similar to Diggerslist, but appeared to have less inventory.

I stared out the windshield, thinking. Gary had a lot of building materials on his back porch. Maybe he was looking to sell some of it. Better than having it clutter up the yard.

I picked up my phone again and called Cal.

"You making progress?" he asked. Right to the point.

I felt like a broken record as I again related all that had recently occurred.

"Wow. You actually saw a dead body? You okay?"

"It smells different than you'd think," I said, sensing the odor in the car. I rubbed my nose. "I've read about it, but now experiencing it, it's like nothing I can describe."

"You want to consider a career change? Your mother would be delighted."

That was true. My parents would love it if I gave up being a detective and got a *real* job. "I don't give up that easily. Besides, I have to find Deuce."

"What can I help with?"

"Has anyone else called his cell phone?"

"That would be a negative. At least since this morning."

"Okay, keep checking. Another thing: would you be able to get onto Craigslist and see if Gary placed any ads there?"

"That's a weird request. What rabbit trail are you going on?"

"It's probably nothing, but Gary has a bunch of stuff on his back porch, like electrical wiring, copper pipes, and rebar. And he had a list of websites, including Craigslist, on a notepad in his bedroom. It makes sense he's selling the stuff."

"So?"

"Maybe someone killed him over that stuff."

"That's a bit thin, don't you think? Is anything valuable?"

"I don't know," I said. "Copper's worth a lot right now. I'll bet the pipes lying around would make him a pretty penny."

"Enough to kill someone over it?"

"I don't know," I said.

"Maybe there's more stuff in the garage. Did you check?"

"No, I was a bit sidetracked...you know, by the body."

"Oh yeah," Cal said. "So, if we follow this theory of yours, we need to find out if Gary was selling his leftover materials. Which brings us back to Craigslist."

"Yes."

"You know how Craigslist works, right?"

"Sure," I said. "You place an online ad and people contact you."

"Yeah, but you don't typically email the person placing the ad. The emails go through the Craigslist servers so the users are anonymous. It's safer that way."

"Unless Gary put his name, phone number, or email in the ad itself."

"He'd be stupid to do so, but if that happened, I can do a search on the ads and find one."

"If not, wouldn't Craigslist have some record of Gary's real email?"

"Absolutely. So I'd need to find Gary's email."

"Can you?" I asked.

"I'll give it a shot."

"And one more thing."

"That isn't enough?"

"This is easy," I said. I gave him the license plate of the forest-green truck.

"That's the guy that came to Gary's house while you were there?"

"Yeah. He talked about dumping some stuff, and sounds like he's in cahoots with Gary. He might know who came by Gary's house last night."

"You're right, that is an easy request."

"Can you do it? Now?"

"Hang on a second." I heard clicking. His fingers on the keyboard. "It's a truck registered to Shane Mundy. He's twenty."

"Address?"

He rattled it off and I jotted it down.

"Great. I'm going to run by Shane's and see if he's there." I glanced at the clock on the dashboard. It was now after two in the afternoon. "And I'm going to get some lunch. Can you do a little more research on Shane, see if you can find anything interesting?"

"Will do. I call you in a while."

I thanked him, hung up, and drove off.

CHAPTER SEVENTEEN

I stopped at a Subway for a meatball sub. As I wolfed it down, I thought about where things were going. Somehow Deuce was tied to Gary, but I didn't know how. And Shane was tied to Gary, but I didn't know how. I hoped by the time I figured it out, it wouldn't be too late for Deuce. It was as bad as *The Big Sleep*, with its convoluted plot.

Shane Mundy rented an apartment near Broadway and Dartmouth, about six miles directly south of downtown Denver. The building was like many others in the area, a three-story L-shape with a tiny parking lot, and no extra amenities like a pool or workout room. Shane lived on the third floor.

I scanned the lot and the surrounding streets, but didn't see his truck. I was debating what to do next when my phone rang.

"Shane works at Criss Cross Construction," Cal said without any ado.

"I should've known. All these guys know each other. And I'll bet that means he knows Deuce, too."

"Uh huh."

"How'd you find that out?"

"Let's just say I tracked down his banking information and traced back the direct deposits from Criss Cross."

"I don't want to know how you did it all," I said. How Cal never got caught, I don't know.

"Did you find out anything about Craigslist?"

"Negativo, but I'm still working on it."

"Okay," I said. "I'm going to see if I can track Shane down at Criss Cross."

"What if he works at a different site from where Deuce did?"

"Good question." I paused. "I'm stabbing in the dark right now."

"I'll see if I can find out," Cal said. "Oh, and still no calls to Deuce's cell phone."

"Thanks. I'll talk to you later."

I sat in the car for a minute, debating what to do. Criss Cross Construction had multiple job sites. How could I find out which one Shane worked at? I could go back to the main headquarters, but I doubted that Lon Carlson's secretary, Edna, would be thrilled to see me. I looked at the clock on the dashboard: 3:15. By the time I drove over there, it would be close to four. Somehow I didn't think Edna would want to let me see Carlson again today. And I didn't have time to wait. But there was another place I could try.

I put the 4Runner in gear and headed back downtown to the Vanguard site. Chuck Fitzhugh had been pleasant with me this morning, and I figured if he knew where Shane worked, he'd tell me.

I turned on to 15th Street and approached the entrance to the building site. I was about to turn into the lot when I spied a blue Mustang parked in front of the trailer. I swore. Detective

Sarah Spillman was there, presumably telling Fitzhugh about Gary, and asking questions. Not a good time to drop in and ask about Shane.

I drove past the entrance, around the block and then parked where I could see the trailer. I'd have to talk to Fitzhugh after she left. I hoped it wouldn't be too long, but that was the life of a detective. It wasn't like in the movies, with nonstop action. I sat back in my seat and cranked the tunes. I tapped my fingers on the steering wheel along with the Violent Femmes.

Right at five o'clock, the secretary I'd met this morning came out of the trailer and walked to a Toyota Prius. She got in and a moment later drove out of the lot, followed by a white truck. Quitting time, I thought as another car turned onto the street. And then a forest-green truck appeared.

I perked up, squinting to see the license plate or the driver. Young with a goatee. Bingo! It was Shane.

The truck waited for an opening in traffic and then it turned onto 15th and drove off. I whipped a U-turn and fell into place behind him, letting a couple of cars get in between us. The truck was big and easy to keep in view, and Shane wasn't in any hurry, driving with the flow of traffic. I doubt he had any clue he was being followed.

He soon turned on California and headed past the convention center and onto Colfax. I had no idea where he was going.

We stayed on Colfax, drove past the Auraria College Campus, and then Shane exited onto Interstate 25. He took that north to 58th, then got off and made his way east, where he turned on a side street that was lined with businesses, ranging from tires to construction. He drove to Paxton Electric and parked near a side entrance. I stopped down the block where I could keep the truck in view.

Shane hopped out and went inside the building. A minute

later, he came out a side entrance, followed by a gangly guy in jeans and a red baseball cap. I grabbed a pair of binoculars from the back seat and trained it on them.

They strolled to Shane's truck and stood beside it, chatting for a moment. Then Shane went to the tailgate, let it down, and started taking bales of wiring from the back. As he unloaded them, the red-capped fellow grabbed the bales and hauled them inside the building.

In a few minutes they finished and the man took cash out of his pocket and handed it to Shane. Shane counted it and they shook hands. They chatted a moment longer, then Shane got back into the truck, waved, and drove out of the parking lot. He headed back to the highway, still seemingly unaware that I was behind him.

I now had Shane selling building materials, I thought as I kept the truck in front of me. Where did he get the wiring? From Gary? If so, where did Gary get it? Were they buying wholesale, marking the price up, and then selling it? Or were they stealing it? How could I find out? And the biggest question was, how did Deuce fit into all this?

I mulled this over, my mind on autopilot as we crawled along the highway. We passed downtown Denver and then Shane exited on Santa Fe and then onto Evans. The neighborhood changed and it dawned on me where we were going. A few minutes later, Shane turned onto Acoma. He slowed down in front of Gary's house. Then he gunned the engine and the truck squealed off down the street. I drove by the house and saw yellow crime-scene tape strung across the door. That must've spooked Shane.

I sped up to the corner and saw the truck make a left back onto Broadway. I fell in behind again and followed Shane north to a bar near downtown on Platte Street. He parked in one of a few spots in front, got out, slammed the door, and strode into the bar. I parked across the street, waited a minute, and then went inside.

CHAPTER EIGHTEEN

Platte Street Bar & Grill was decent-sized, dimly lit, with four booths along the front windows, a long bar along the back wall, and a number of small tables in between. Two pool tables sat in a back room. Music played from that room, drifting into the main room. It was loud, but not so much to drown out conversation.

I stood in the doorway for a moment, looking around. A stocky waitress with a nose ring approached, carrying a tray with four longneck Budweisers balanced on her tattooed arm.

"You can sit anywhere," she said with a nod at the tables.

I returned the nod and took a couple of slow steps, trying to find Shane. I spotted him sitting in the third booth, the neon light from a Coors sign in the window tinting his face blue. I raised a hand and scratched my head, trying to shield my face as I slid into the booth next to his, my back to him. I sat forward and could see his reflection in the window. He was fiddling with his beer bottle, ripping the label off it. He still didn't have a clue that I'd been tailing him.

"Whatcha want?" The stocky waitress stood at my table,

brushing off a tee shirt with Platte Street Bar & Grill on it. I was so focused on Shane, I hadn't noticed her approach.

"I'll take a Fat Tire," I said.

"Sure thing, honey."

She stepped over to Shane's booth. He mumbled something and she sauntered away.

The occasional crack of colliding pool balls filtered in from the other room. I wished I was in there playing. The waitress brought my Fat Tire and delivered another beer to Shane. I nursed my beer; not knowing how long I'd have to wait, I needed a clear head. People drifted in and out, some sitting at tables and eating dinner, others heading straight to the pool tables. It seemed a popular hangout with the blue-collar set, as I saw a lot of guys in jeans and work boots. I glanced in the window again. Shane was drinking fast, slamming down three more beers in quick succession.

Just before six a muscular man with dark, spiky hair entered the bar. He took off sunglasses and hooked them on his shirt as he looked around. I cursed under my breath. It was the guy from the concrete company that I'd run into this morning at the Vanguard job site.

From behind me I heard, "Matt, over here."

I turned and focused on the window. The man walked past my booth, not giving me a second glance. I let out a breath of relief.

"You said we needed to talk," Matt said as he slid into the booth. "What's up?"

I felt the back of my seat give a little with his weight.

"Man, do you have any idea what's going on?" Shane's voice was strained and he was talking loud. Easy to hear over the music.

"What're you talking about? Everything's fine."

"Nah, man. You're not at Vanguard so you don't know what's going on."

They paused while the waitress came over. Matt ordered a Coors.

"What are you talking about?" he asked when the waitress walked away.

"After I left Gary's today, I went back to work," Shane said. "And later this afternoon, the cops came by to talk to Chuck."

"About what?"

"I didn't know at the time, but then I went back by Gary's. Man, there's crime-scene tape on the door!"

"So?"

"And Gary didn't show up to work. He's dead, man. Dead!"

"Calm down," Matt said. "You don't know that."

"Yeah, I do. Some of the guys called me and they said somebody shot Gary."

Matt was quiet as the waitress brought his beer. "You okay, honey?" the waitress asked as she passed by my booth.

I nodded distractedly, focused on the conversation behind me.

"Someone's figured out what we're doing," Shane said.

"Don't be ridiculous. No one has any idea."

"Then why is Gary dead?"

"Gary's a scumbag. Everyone hates him. Maybe some ex-girlfriend killed him."

"You know that ain't it."

Glass rattled.

"Calm down!" Matt said again.

I leaned forward and peered at the window reflection. Shane had knocked some of the empty bottles over.

Matt moved them out of the way, thumping them loudly on the table. "You're overreacting," he said.

"Nah, this ain't right. Someone's onto us. I want out. I'm done." Shane nervously pulled at his goatee.

Matt's voice grew lower, and it had a sharp, dangerous edge to it. "You're not going anywhere. I need your help tomorrow, and you're gonna to do it."

"What if I don't?"

"I'll call the cops and tell them about you."

"Go on ahead, and I'll tell them about you."

Matt laughed. "You think the cops are going to believe you? You're twenty and you've already been arrested more times than I can count, busted for DUI's *and* possession. They'll believe *you* over me? Get real."

Shane stared out the window, his face twisted into an angry mask. I averted my gaze, even though I knew he wasn't looking toward me. After a moment, I glanced back at their reflections. Shane had turned back to Matt.

"Fine, I'll help. But what if the cops come back? What if they want to talk to me?"

"Why?"

"They might know that Gary and I hang out."

"Did you kill Gary?"

"What? Of course not."

"Then you tell them that. And that's it. Nothing about anything else."

"But —"

"Nothing else. If you do, you'll have me to answer to."

Matt's tone left little doubt that he would back up what he said. "You get my meaning?" he asked.

"I won't say nothin'," Shane said sullenly.

"Good. I'd hate to see you end up like Gary."

"What's that supposed to mean?"

Matt stared down Shane. "Forget it," he finally said.

Shane tensed, frowning. Then he eyed Matt warily. "What about the stuff at Gary's?" he asked. "We can't get it now."

Matt grunted. "We'll have to leave it. Too bad. There's a nice chunk of change there. Oh, by the way, where's the money?"

Shane pulled a wad of cash from his pocket and handed it across the table. Matt counted it, then peeled off a few bills and tossed them back at Shane.

"There's your cut," he said. He picked up his beer, drained it, and set the bottle back on the table. "I'm out of here." He slid from the booth and stood up. I stayed still, my head turned away from him. "Just keep your mouth shut and everything will be fine. I'll see you tomorrow night."

Matt left the bar without looking back. Just then, my cell phone rang. I grabbed it from my pocket. It was Bob, most likely calling for an update. What timing! I silenced it just as Shane stormed past me.

I had a quick decision to make: Follow them outside so I could see if they said anything more in the parking lot, but risk being discovered, or stay put until they got in their cars. I opted for the latter.

I leaned close to the window and put a hand against the glass to cut down the glare. Shane was just outside the door, lighting a cigarette. Matt was at the street, getting into a gray truck. I was too far away to read the license plate, but I did notice a logo painted on the door. I couldn't quite make it out but I thought there were circles on it. Kind of like what Linda described. Was it Matt who was at Gary's last night? He threatened Shane. Did he threaten Gary as well, and then it got out of hand?

I didn't have time to think about it because Shane was on the move again. I threw some bills on the table and hurried out of the bar. Shane was in his truck, backing out. The sun was setting, taking with it its warmth, and purple and orange hues streaked the western sky. I darted behind Shane's truck and walked to my 4Runner. By the time I got started, his truck was halfway down the street.

His driving was a little more erratic, probably due to the three or four beers he'd downed. I stayed with him as he stopped at a liquor store for more beer and to a McDonald's drive-through. Then he went home, climbing the stairs to his apartment without a look back.

"Some kind of crook," I muttered as I waited across the street. "Doesn't have a clue that he's been followed since he left work."

I waited a while, debating what to do. I could stay and see if Shane went back out. But since he had his dinner and more beer, I didn't think that would happen, so I decided to go home. I'd pick up the surveillance tomorrow.

CHAPTER NINETEEN

I got up at four the next morning. I wasn't thrilled with the prospect of tailing Shane again, but I needed to know more about what he and his buddy Matt were up to, and I had to know what he and Matt had planned for this evening.

I stopped at a Starbucks, bought coffee and an apple fritter, and then headed to Shane's. I wanted to get there plenty early so I could catch him leaving. Traffic was light and I made it to his place shortly before five, so I ended up waiting for quite a while. At six-thirty, right about the time the coffee had run through me, Shane emerged from his apartment. He walked with his head down, shoulders drooped, a man with a heavy burden. Given everything I'd seen and heard yesterday, I could understand why.

Shane drove directly to the Vanguard job site, parked in the lot, donned a hardhat, and disappeared somewhere in the building. I took the opportunity to relieve myself at a café down the block, then came back to the 4-Rrunner and moved it to a paid lot for the day.

Trucks and cars drove in and out as the workday progressed.

I donned a light jacket to ward off the cool morning air and walked around the block, carrying a Canon camera with a zoom lens in a leather bag. As I watched the goings-on, I spied Shane working with a crew on the skeleton of the building. I took out the Canon, focused in on him, and snapped a couple of good shots, with a much higher resolution at that distance than what I could get with my cell phone camera. Since he looked to be occupied for a while, I took the opportunity to grab breakfast at the café. I loitered a while, watching out the window, and then I went outside and sat on the edge of a planter in the sun. After a while, it warmed up and I took off my jacket. No one seemed bothered by my presence.

A little after eleven, I spotted Matt walking toward the office trailer. I hadn't notice him coming in, but I perked up now. A moment later, Fitzhugh emerged from the trailer. They stood talking for a few minutes. Then Shane appeared.

I took the camera, zoomed in on them, and shot pictures as they chatted. After a few minutes, Fitzhugh and Matt went into the office. Shane walked out the gate and to the corner, where he bought a hotdog from a street vendor. As he walked back to the job site, he hooked up with a few other workers, and they strolled back inside.

It wasn't until their workday ended that things picked up – more than I would've preferred.

––––––

At five Shane left work with everyone else and drove back to Platte Street Bar & Grill. I thought I'd be pushing my luck if I went inside again, so I waited in the 4Runner across the street. An hour later, Shane came out, drove to McDonald's and ate, and then returned to the Vanguard job site which, by this time, was deserted. Shane parked in front of the gate, got out and unlocked it, and drove in. A moment later the truck vanished around the corner of the building.

I pulled into a space across the street, snatched the camera from the passenger seat, and hopped out. Angry black clouds threatened a storm. As if to validate this, thunder rumbled overhead. I fed the meter and dodged cars as I crossed the street. I approached the gate and looked around. I didn't see anyone around the office trailer, nor was there anybody around the skeleton of the building. I listened for sounds from within the site, but the din of traffic behind me drowned out anything I might've heard. I glanced around once more, then walked through the gate, acting as if I had every right to be there. I kept close to the high-rise structure, holding my camera at my side. I had no idea what I'd say if I ran into anyone. I reached the end of the building and glanced around the corner.

Shane's truck sat on the other side of a large concrete floor, but I didn't see him. I waited a second, then slipped around the corner of the building and moved along the side of it. Five steps later, I spotted Shane. He was on the other side of the truck, cutting apart bundles of rebar. He turned around and I dove to the left, crouching behind a pile of wooden pallets stacked by a steel pillar.

Shane stood for a second, staring in my direction. I was sure he'd seen me. I peeked between the wood slats of a pallet. My heart pounded as I watched him look around. A few big drops of rain pelted down. He glanced up at the ominous sky, then shrugged and picked up a bundle of rebar and heaved it in the bed of the truck. He worked hard, but the rebar was heavy and he stopped periodically to rest. As he worked, I took pictures. After half an hour, he had nearly filled the truck. The mist morphed quickly to rain, and I knew it was time to go. I'd tail him again when he drove out.

I backed away and was almost to the edge of the building

when a flash of lightning streaked across the sky and a split-second later, thunder boomed. I hit the ground, cradling the camera in my hands, and looked over my shoulder. Shane was staring right in my direction. I didn't move a muscle. He continued to stare into the gloom, then finally went back to his truck.

I crawled around the corner, stood up, and dashed through the rain to the 4Runner. I hadn't even caught my breath when Shane's truck drove back through the entrance. He hopped out and as he locked the gate, he stared both left and right. I sank down into the seat so he wouldn't see me. He rushed back to the truck, glanced around again, and then drove off.

I followed at a safe distance, aware that Shane was now suspicious. Rain poured on us for a few minutes, and then subsided as we drove west, where the storm had already passed through. The ground and streets were wet, and the sky had turned an inky black as darkness fell.

While I kept pace with Shane, I called Cal.

"What's up?" he asked.

"I've got Shane in my sights. He just loaded up a bunch of rebar from the Vanguard job site and now he's taking it out west."

"So they're stealing stuff and selling it."

"Sure looks that way. I saw him sell some wiring to an electrical company yesterday."

"And you've got Gary selling stuff on eBay," Cal said.

"You found ads?"

"Yep. He's been selling wiring, copper piping and more."

"How much do you think he made?"

"It's hard to say, but a good bit if he's been doing this for a while. I looked up half-inch up to one-inch pipes. Ones that are ten feet long go from about twenty-five bucks to sixty per pipe."

I thought about the stack of pipes on Gary's back porch. "He's making good money then," I said, "because he had a stack of pipes on his back porch, along with other materials. You combine that with selling to other companies, who knows how much they're pulling in."

"Not bad."

I sighed. "I just can't believe Deuce is involved in all this."

"It's not like him," Cal said. "Or maybe he found out what was going on and was going to tell."

"And somebody stopped him from doing so," I said. "That sounds more like him."

"Think one of these guys will lead you to him?"

"I hope so."

"When I find out where Shane's headed, I'll know more."

I soon knew Shane's destination: McClellan Concrete Construction. It was tucked into a residential neighborhood off of Colfax and Sheridan, in Lakewood. Shane turned south into the parking lot and I continued on west, past an area full of machinery and supplies. An eight-foot high chain-link fence surrounded the property, which extended almost to the end of a long block. I went halfway down the next block, parked, grabbed a small flashlight, and ran back through the darkness. A small field backed up to the west side of the property, and as I approached the fence, Shane's truck was pulling into a space between two cement trucks and stacks of bricks.

The streetlight across the road did little to illuminate the field, and I crawled slowly along the fence through high, wet weeds. Shane had left his headlights on and they shone on an area where he was unloading the rebar. I stopped twenty feet away, near the cement trucks, and watched, wondering why I was out in the cold and wet instead of in my car.

"Hurry up."

Matt's voice made me jump.

Shane cursed. Apparently he'd been surprised, too. "Why don't you help?"

"All right."

Matt appeared in the headlights as he moved around the truck. "What took you so long?"

"This stuff's heavy!" Shane grunted. "And besides, I think someone was watching me."

"Would you relax! Everything's fine."

"I don't know. I'm telling you, man, I want out."

"I'm getting tired of your whining, Shane."

"What's that supposed to mean?"

"Forget it. Let's get this finished."

They worked in silence. Matt climbed into the truck bed and shoved rebar out onto the ground while Shane worked to stack it up beside some other materials.

"Okay, I've kept some back," Matt said as he jumped off the back of the truck.

Shane stopped and nodded.

"You'll get your cut from this after I sell it later this week," Matt said as he pointed to the stacks that they'd unloaded. "You sell the stuff in the truck and keep the money."

"Okay," Shane agreed.

"I don't know why you're so worried," Matt said. "You're double-dipping and making some nice extra change."

"Uh huh." Shane didn't sound convinced.

They're stealing from Criss Cross Construction, and then stealing from the stealings, I thought.

"I've got some work to do in the office before I lock up. Get that stuff stacked and then get out of here."

"Don't forget the alarm," Shane laughed.

"I've got a night guard, what do I need an alarm for?"

"It was a joke. I know about the night guard," Shane said sarcastically.

"Oh." Matt shrugged, the joke obviously flying over his head. He shook his head at Shane and then strode off.

As Shane finished stacking the rebar, I could hear him talking to himself.

"I gotta get out of this, man. It ain't worth the money."

The crisp night air filled with his cursing. A few minutes later, he finished. He kicked the last of the rebar, got in his truck and drove off.

I stayed crouched down, my fingers intertwined in the fence. I now knew they were stealing from Criss Cross Construction, but how could I prove it? It was too dark to take pictures, and even so, that would only show them unloading materials. It wouldn't prove they stole anything. And where was Deuce? I wondered if I could find some paperwork in the office that would incriminate Matt and his buddies. Regardless, I couldn't do anything more where I was. I stood up, stretched my stiff legs, and walked back through the field and down the street to the 4Rrunner. I got in, started it, and drove slowly with my headlights off. As I neared the entrance to McClellan Concrete Construction, I pulled to the curb and turned off the engine. I could follow Matt, but I wasn't sure what that would get me. I could take a chance that the building didn't have an alarm, as Matt alluded to, and break in and see what I could find inside the offices, avoiding the night guard. Not an easy task, but possible. Or I could go home now.

I tapped the steering wheel, thinking it over. Then I hunkered down and waited for Matt to leave.

CHAPTER TWENTY

A little before nine, the front door to McClellan Concrete Construction opened. A rectangular patch of soft yellow light cut into the darkness, and a second later Matt emerged. He drove out of the lot, stopping long enough to secure a large swinging metal gate with a lock and chain.

I waited a minute, and when all stayed quiet, grabbed my set of lock picks and got out of the 4Rrunner. I quietly closed the door, went to the fence, and listened. Satisfied no one was around, I climbed the fence, balanced at the top for a second, then lowered myself on the other side. I ran across the empty parking lot and up a short flight of steps to the front door. I gazed inside a narrow window to the left of double doors to see if I could spot an alarm system. It was logical that it would be near the door so that whoever entered could quickly turn it off before the alarm sounded. Not seeing anything, I decided to move ahead. I took out my lock picks and set to work on the door.

On a previous case, I'd had to have Cal break into a house using a set of lock picks. He hadn't been thrilled when things took a dangerous turn, and after that particular case, he'd shown me how to pick locks so he wouldn't have to help with that task again.

After a minute or two of fiddling, I was about to give up, wondering how Cal made it look so easy. Then the lock gave and I opened the door. I stepped inside, bracing myself for a screeching alarm. Nothing. I didn't see a system anywhere around, nor did I hear the telltale beeping many alarms make when the door opens. Unless there was some kind of hidden, silent alarm, I was safe.

I took out my flashlight and switched it on. I was on a landing with half-flights of stairs that led up and down. I chose up, tiptoeing as I climbed the stairs. To my right was a reception area, with a desk and chair, a short couch and a coffee table with magazines on it, and beyond it, a long hallway. A couple of recessed ceiling lights were on, leaving the hall dimly lit.

I walked past the reception area and noticed a short hallway to my left with a door to an office, and down another set of stairs, a door that led outside. I glanced in the office. The name on the door read "Matt McClellan". Hmm. He was important enough to have a nameplate on the door. *Very important person?* I wondered. I stepped inside, closed the door and shone the light around the room.

Along the wall to my right were three metal file cabinets. On the opposite wall sat a desk that faced the room. Pictures of construction sites hung along the third wall, and on the other, a large window looked out at a chain-link fence. Past that was a ravine and then a ranch-style house. I shielded the flashlight with my hand, hoping no one outside would notice it. I went to the desk. It had the usual accoutrements: computer, phone, 'In' and 'Out' trays, and piles of paper, files, and legal notepads. A little model truck held business cards. I picked up one and read it. Turns out Matt McClellan was the president of McClellan

Concrete Construction. And he was stealing from Criss Cross Construction. Interesting. Now I needed to find proof of it.

I stuffed a card in my pocket, then rummaged around the papers, not sure what I was looking for. I sat down and began reading the papers but came up with nothing. I went over to the file cabinets and opened the left one. Inside were files for various jobs. I found a file for Criss Cross Construction, opened it, and scanned the documents. There was an invoice for rebar, but the numbers meant nothing, other than the bill was thousands of dollars. I thumbed through more, then stopped and listened. Did I hear something? Must be my imagination. Regardless, I needed to hurry. I pulled out the invoice for the rebar, shined the flashlight on it, and snapped a picture with my phone. I put the file back and then paused again. I stood still for a second, then went to the door. I put my ear against it, my hand on the doorknob. I swear I was hearing something.

I flicked off the flashlight, turned the knob and carefully opened the door, half expecting Matt to be there. I was wrong.

Instead, a big black Rottweiler stood ten feet down the hallway, panting at me. One eye was glazed over and his snout was flecked with gray.

"Ha ha, the night guard," I muttered. A huge drooling guard dog. What a cliché.

Then the cliché growled at me, baring a number of large teeth at me.

"Nice doggy," I said, my mind racing through options.

Jump back into the office and close the door? That would make for an interesting conversation when the receptionist arrived. *I was taking pictures of your invoices when I ran into your very impressive guard dog, so I thought I'd relax here until morning.* No, that wouldn't do.

Try and take him out – but how? Throw my flashlight or

lock picks at him? He'd probably think they were snacks. No again.

Run past him to the front door? The Rottweiler growled again and lowered his head. No, I'd never make it that far. That left the back door.

I glanced over. It had a deadbolt that I'd have to unlock. Precious seconds to do that. A noise interrupted my thoughts. The front door had opened.

"It's time to get rid of Shane. He's a loose cannon and I don't like it."

Matt had come back! I had no idea who he was talking to, and right at that moment I didn't care. The Rottweiler jerked his head toward the voice and I acted. I leaped down the stairs and slammed into the door. I flipped the deadbolt, wrenched open the door and stumbled outside, the Rottweiler snarling as he bounded after me.

Matt yelled, his voice cut off by the slamming door. The Rottweiler barked furiously as he hit the closing door, then bounded out. I jumped halfway up the fence and clawed my way to the top just as the dog hurtled himself toward me. His jaws clamped down on my calf. I swore, shook my leg violently and he let go, taking a piece of my jeans with him. Adrenaline surged through me as I hoisted my body up, then swung myself over the fence. I dropped, landing in a heap on the other side, tumbling head over heels down the ravine.

Behind me, I heard Matt hollering at the dog. I scrambled to my feet and tore down the ravine, stumbling in the dark until I reached a clump of underbrush still wet from the earlier rain. I pitched myself behind it, crouched down and wheezed, trying to catch my breath. I stared back at the building. Up the slope, Matt stood on the other side of the fence, silhouetted by a light over the door, the dog panting beside him.

"Who's out there?" Matt said.

I gasped for breath, a stitch in my side. Then I became aware of pain in my leg. It throbbed and burned. I winced, gritting my teeth.

"Your bad luck I came back," Matt said, brandishing a metal rod. He started down the fence, his arm outstretched, the rod clicking on the fence. The dog followed, snarling. Matt stopped about twenty feet from me, at the limit of the light's illumination. He stood for a long time, staring into the gloom, head cocked, listening. The dog wandered closer to my hiding place. Matt whacked the fence and the dog stopped a few feet from me, glaring through the fence.

"Can't see shit," Matt finally muttered. He whistled but the dog stayed put. "Hey!" he hollered. "Damn deaf dog. I swear, you're old and useless."

The dog trudged back to Matt, and they walked back to the building, pausing at the door. Matt wrenched it open angrily, held the door for the dog, and disappeared inside. A moment later, the light winked out.

I hadn't realized I'd been holding my breath. I let it out slowly while I waited to see if Matt would come back out. I was tempted to stay put until I heard Matt's truck leave, but I couldn't take the chance that he'd call the police or come hunting for me. So I stood up and limped up the other side of the ravine and onto the street. I limp-trotted to the end of the block, then on around the back perimeter of McClellan Concrete Construction, careful to avoid the streetlights. Less than five minutes later, I came around the front side of the property. I kept my eye on the front door of the building. Matt's truck was parked in the space right by the front door, but he was nowhere to be seen. I hurried to the 4Runner, got in, and drove away.

I wish I could say I breathed easier, but the throbbing in my leg had turned into a fiery ache, and I was noticing other aches and pains. A few blocks from McClellan Concrete Construction, I pulled over, rolled up my pant leg, and looked at my calf. Bite marks where the Rottweiler had sunk his teeth into my leg were angry red and blood oozed from puncture wounds. It wasn't as bad as it could've been, probably because the dog was old and lacking some teeth. But it still needed to be checked. I knew where to go, but I knew one person there who wouldn't be thrilled to see me in my present condition.

CHAPTER TWENTY-ONE

"This isn't the way to win my heart," Willie said as she pushed aside the flimsy curtain and stared at me. I was lying on an emergency room bed, trying hard not to fall asleep. It had been a long day, and I was dirty, wet, and tired. A doctor had already been in and out, saying someone would be back to treat me. That had been a while ago, and I was surprised to see Willie. Even though she was frowning at me, she was still awfully cute in light blue scrubs, a clipboard in her hands, her short blond hair tucked behind her ears.

"Believe me," I said. "I don't want to see you right now either."

"You don't want to see me?" She stared at me, confused.

"No! I just meant," I fumbled for the words. "Not like this. I'd rather be taking you to the movies or something, not coming into the hospital because I'm hurt."

On another occasion I'd been brought to Denver Health for treatment, and Willie had been working that night. It was not a highlight of my career, and it had done little to allay Willie's fears about the dangers of my profession.

As if to confirm that, she said, "I'd rather not see you here either."

"I thought you were off today," I said. I sat up and slowly swung my legs over the side of the bed, wincing at the pain in my leg.

"The shift opened up, so I took it. Better than sitting around worrying about you."

The sarcasm was clearly evident. I shrugged my shoulders. "I wasn't *planning* on getting hurt." I grimaced. "Believe me, I wasn't."

"No one ever does," she snapped.

I stared at her, surprised by her tone. "What does that mean?"

She frowned. "My dad would say that. 'I don't plan on getting hurt.' But it doesn't help you from worrying. And he had some close calls."

I put a hand on her shoulder. "Like what?"

"When I was eight years old, he stopped an armed robbery in progress. The robber shot at my dad. The bullet...it just missed his head."

"That must've been horrible."

"It was," she said. "That was the first close call. After that, I could never stop worrying about him. And now I can't stop worrying about you."

"I'm sorry," I sighed. "But nothing ever happened to your dad, right? And nothing's going to happen to me."

She nodded, then her face softened. "Dog bite, huh?" She set the clipboard on the bed, sat down on a rolling chair, and gestured with her hand at me. I lifted my leg, resting my foot on her thigh, and she examined the dog bite.

"What happened?"

"The building I was in wasn't supposed to have an alarm system," I said, grimacing again as she touched the area around the wound. "Turns out it did." I told her about breaking into McClellan Concrete Construction and running into the Rottweiler.

"They're stealing from Criss Cross Construction?" Willie asked.

"It sure looks that way. Shane works at Criss Cross, so he can get onto the property after hours. And Gary was in on it, too. Matt seems to be the brains behind the operation. He gets the guys to steal stuff, and they store it at McClellan. Then they sell it off whenever and wherever they can. As an incentive to keep the scheme going, Matt lets Shane and Gary keep some aside. They sell *that* and make a little more."

"And no one's caught them?"

I shook my head. "It's seems too easy, though. I can't believe no one at Criss Cross knows. Maybe they're dealing with so much material, they can't keep track of all this happening under the table." I rubbed a hand through my hair. "I don't know. I must be missing something."

She sat back, a pensive look crossing her face.

"What?" I asked.

"It's weird. When I came on this afternoon I helped with a guy who'd been hurt at a construction site. I overheard him talking to a friend. He was talking about stuff going on under the table, and he said he wondered if the rumors about the rigging were true."

"Did the guy work at Criss Cross?"

"I don't know, but he said something about a high-rise downtown."

"Which one?"

She pursed her lips, thinking. "Does Vanguard mean anything?"

"That's the one. If others know about this, it sounds like Matt and his gang haven't been as careful as they thought."

"What do you think he meant about rigging?" she asked.

I shrugged. "I don't know. Deuce was asking me about that, too, the night he disappeared. I guess you do something with rigging in construction, but I don't know what."

She prodded my leg some more and I flinched.

"Sit still," she ordered. She grabbed gauze pads, hydrogen peroxide and antibiotic ointment from a supply cabinet behind me. Then she prepared soap and water, washed the dog bite, dried it with gauze pads, and cleaned it again with the hydrogen peroxide. She paused at that point, and looked up at me. "What about Deuce?"

"He's been talking to Gary, and he had all that extra money in his room," I said. "He must've been involved."

Willie's face flushed with disappointment. "I just can't believe he'd do something like that."

"Me either. Maybe they tricked him or something." I shook my head. "Oh Deuce, what were you thinking?"

"Do you think Matt killed Gary?" She avoided bringing up Deuce again.

"Maybe. Matt's a dangerous guy, and he wasn't happy that Shane wanted out. Maybe Gary wanted out and Matt took care of him."

She applied antibiotic ointment, then tore open a packet of bandages and taped up my leg. "Or Gary was taking more than his share," she said.

"Could be. There's only one way to find out."

"You have to talk to Matt."

"Afraid so."

Willie didn't look happy, but she also knew I had to do it. She sighed. "Before you do anything else, you might need a rabies shot. Not fun."

I groaned. "Couldn't we skip that?"

"You think the dog guarding that place is safe?"

"Probably not, but do I have to get a rabies shot right now? Can't we wait?" Ah, the tough detective, taken down by a needle.

Willie chuckled, sensing my trepidation. "I talked to the doctor before I came in. You don't have to get the shot now, and since most dogs don't have rabies, we can wait. If we can get the dog's records and verify it's had vaccinations, we don't have to worry. Can you ask the owner?"

The sarcasm was back. I threw her a *ha-ha* look. "I don't think that's possible."

"Tell you what. I'll call McClellan tomorrow and say I'm with animal control and we received a report of a dog biting someone. They'll have to give me the information."

"You'd do that?"

She reached out and grabbed my hands. "I want to help."

I leaned forward and she kissed me, long and lingering. My hands moved around her back, then lower.

"I have to get back to work," she said breathily, breaking away. "I'll come by your place when my shift is over."

I sighed. "One of these days, we won't be interrupted..."

She smoothed the front of her scrubs as I stood up.

"Promise me you'll be careful," she finally said.

I touched my bandaged leg. "You don't have to worry about that."

"I do," I heard her whisper as I limped out of the room.

CHAPTER TWENTY-TWO

Matt McClellan lived in an older part of town, in a small, two-story house in a neighborhood of small, cookie-cutter houses in a Littleton suburb. The yards were large, with mature trees and detached garages toward the back of the properties. It was almost one when I pulled to a stop a few houses down from his.

After I'd left the hospital, I'd run home, where I cleaned up and changed out of my dirty, wet clothes. Then I took a few minutes to find out where Matt lived. For once, I hadn't needed Cal to help me; since I knew Matt's last name, I was able to look up his address on the Internet. Good old White Pages. Armed with that information, and my gun, which I decided to bring with me, I drove to Matt's.

I wasn't sure what I was doing there at this hour. I could knock on the door and confront him, let him know I knew he was stealing materials from Criss Cross and selling it. But proving it was shaky at best, and I'd have to admit I broke into his office. Not something I wanted to do. And if I confronted him, I was tipping my hand that I was on to him. The only way that would be successful is if I could force him to tell me about Deuce. If not, I was screwed.

For the second time that night, I walked stealthily through a dark neighborhood. I'd put on black jeans and tee shirt, and a dark coat to ward off the chill in the fall air. Cal called it my "Navy SEAL" look. I stopped under a towering oak in Matt's front yard and studied the house, my hand in my coat pocket, holding the gun. Through the front window was a living room, and it looked like a light was on in the kitchen, in the back of the house. As I stared inside, I noticed movement. Someone was in the kitchen.

I darted to the side of the house and peered around the corner. Matt, wearing shorts and a tee shirt, came out of a side door. He held something against his chest with one arm as he quietly shut the door. He turned around and I heard a crinkling sound. I then realized what he had: a bag of chips, a plate with something on it, possibly a sandwich, and a bottle. He padded in bare feet to the garage. He paused at a side door for a second, did the balancing act again with the food, then opened up the door and disappeared inside. After a second, yellow light filtered through cracks in a window and I heard voices.

Did he have Deuce in there? Was he bringing him food?

I snuck down the driveway and paused at the corner of the garage. The voices grew louder. I sidled up to the garage wall and started toward the window. And the door opened.

I froze, then turned to run.

"Hey!"

Footsteps pounded behind me as I bolted down the driveway. I felt fire in my sore leg with each step, so I was slower than usual. That's better than admitting I was slower than Matt, who tackled me from behind. We crashed to the ground, both of us cursing.

"I got you!" He swore as he punched me in the face.

My head rocked back, but I managed to connect a left, and he grunted. We rolled around, his arms flailing at me. I pushed at him with one hand as I fumbled for my gun, still in my coat pocket. I finally yanked it out and pressed it into his left temple. His hands fell to his sides and he stared at me, hatred in his eyes.

"Stop or I'll call the police!" I snarled, struggling to untangle myself while keeping the gun trained on him. I was on my knees, the gun still on him. As a welt grew under my eye, anger welled up in me. Matt might be dangerous, but I was tired, hurt, and frustrated. That made me dangerous, too.

"Go ahead! You're trespassing," he said, summoning a dose of bravado.

"And you're stealing from Criss Cross Construction."

He tensed, but a cautious look flashed on his face.

"Who the hell are you?" he finally asked.

"I'm a private detective and I'm looking for my friend Deuce Smith. He's missing, but then you know that. Is he in the garage?"

"Who?"

"Deuce." I jerked my head at the garage. "I heard voices. Is he in there?"

Matt spit out a harsh laugh. "It's my man cave, you moron. I was watching television."

I ignored the insult and eyed him carefully as I stood up. I waved the gun at him, indicating he should get up. "Slowly," I said. He pushed himself up, then raised his hands in front of him.

"Don't shoot," he said, a nervous shiver in his voice.

"Let's go," I said, keeping him in front of me. "Back inside the garage."

We walked to the side door, with Matt at an angle where he could still see me.

"Limping, huh?" he said as he turned the knob.

"Shut up."

"Run into Rosie?" he asked.

"Who?"

"Rosie. My Rottweiler."

I glanced at my leg, thinking about the dog. *Rosie?* That dog was a lot of things, but 'rosie' wasn't one of them.

"You broke into my office. That's a crime."

I didn't say anything to that. "Inside." He went through the door. I took a quick look around. The neighborhood was still quiet. I noticed my hands were shaking and I steeled myself as I followed Matt.

The garage had indeed been turned into a man cave. Along one wall was a bar, complete with neon beer signs hanging behind it. A pinball machine sat in a corner and a couch was positioned in front of a large-screen television. A Colorado Rockies baseball game was on. The bag of chips, a plate with bread crumbs on it, and an empty beer bottle sat on a coffee table. But no Deuce.

"I taped the game," Matt said, nodding at the TV. "I was having a quick snack and then I was headed to bed."

In different circumstances I might've been embarrassed. But I was so tired of chasing these guys around, and getting lied to and bit by a dog, that I didn't care. I fixed a hard gaze on him.

"I know what you and Shane and Gary are doing. I've witnessed your operation, and I've got pictures," I said. Matt paled. "But right now I don't care about any of that. Just tell me where Deuce is, and I'll walk away."

Matt threw up his hands. "Who the hell is Deuce?"

"Don't give me that," I said. "Just tell me where he is and I'll walk away."

"I'm telling you, I don't know anything about Deuce."

I took a few quick steps, closing in on him and pointing the gun in his face.

"Okay, you're right." Matt backed up and fell onto the couch. "We've been taking some stuff from Criss Cross. Gary and Shane help take it and sell it. But I don't know anything about your friend, I swear."

I leaned down, grabbed the front of his shirt and put the gun to his forehead.

"What'd you do to Gary?"

"Nothing! I swear!"

"Don't lie to me! You were at Gary's on Sunday night and the next day he's dead."

Matt shrank into his tee shirt, puzzled. "What? Sunday? I wasn't there."

"Yeah, you were, and I have a witness," I said, thinking of Linda.

Matt shook his head vehemently. "I was here, watching football."

"Yeah, right."

"It's true. My wife was watching the game with me, then we went to bed."

I hesitated. "Tell me where Deuce is," I finally said, a menace in my tone that I didn't know I had.

"I don't know!" He winced in pain as I pressed down on the barrel of the gun. "I'm telling the truth."

His eyes pleaded with me to believe him. I straightened up and let him go. He sat back, rubbing his forehead.

"How about I call the police and you can tell them you don't know anything about where Deuce is."

"Go ahead," he said, some of the bravado returning. "You tell them about me, I tell them about you breaking into my office."

He had me there. If I called the police, I could end up in

jail, needing to get bailed out. It would take time away from searching for Deuce. And if Matt *did* know about Deuce, would he clam up? Then where would I be?

"If I find out you're lying to me about Deuce..." I aimed the gun at him again.

"I'm telling the truth. I don't know about your friend!" The fear returned.

I turned and ran out of the garage.

CHAPTER TWENTY-THREE

My hands shook as I clutched the steering wheel. I'd pointed a gun at someone only once before, but I'd never threatened someone like I'd just done to Matt. Bogie was so cool when he faced danger. Light up a cigarette, take a swig of scotch, and he was fine. Myself, I needed some Pepto-Bismol. I couldn't seem to get my adrenaline under control.

I made it home without getting sick and slowly climbed the stairs to my condo. I suddenly felt weary; I wanted to crawl into bed and sleep for hours. I let myself in and then paused. Something didn't seem right. I fingered the gun in my coat pocket, and took a couple cautious steps forward.

"Hey, handsome," Willie said, coming out of the bedroom. She was wearing a shirt of mine, that sexy way that women wear men's shirts, and she was toweling her hair dry.

I relaxed. "Hey, yourself."

"Are you okay?" she asked.

"Uh huh." My mood had drastically changed...for the better.

"How's your leg?"

I walked over to her. "It's okay."

"What happened to your face?" she said, reaching up and gently touching the welt.

"It's fine," I said. "Nothing that a hot shower and you can't take care of."

"Are those simultaneous or one and then the other?"

"How about both?"

"You are incorrigible," she said as she took my hand and led me to the shower.

———

"If Matt's telling the truth, then who was at Gary's?"

It was a while later and we were lying in bed. I'd finally had a chance to tell Willie everything and she was both curious and concerned.

"I think Matt *was* at Gary's, and I think he's lying. And he was damn good at it. But I've got pictures of him and I'm going to show them to Linda. She can confirm that she saw him, and I'll have him."

"Where's Deuce?"

I yawned. "I wish I knew. Once I nail Matt, hopefully he'll tell me what happened to Deuce."

Willie snuggled close to me. "Reed, what if Deuce..."

"Don't say it. We have to be positive."

I held her close. We lay in silence and soon her breathing became even. Exhaustion washed over me and I fell asleep, too.

———

Wednesday dawned with a crispness in the air, and I felt that chill in my mind as I worried about Deuce. I left Willie sleeping, took my camera and laptop, and drove to my office. I hadn't been there since last Friday, so I needed to check my phone messages and take care of the mail. "Ferguson Detective Agency" is two small rooms in a renovated warehouse near my condo. I pay too much for rent, but I love being close to home and the Sixteenth Street Mall, downtown Denver's urban center.

I took the stairs to the second floor, unlocked my office door, and grabbed the mail. I flipped through the envelopes as I crossed to the inner office. Nothing of importance was in the mail, so I tossed it on the desk, then fired up my laptop.

I spent a few minutes transferring the pictures I'd taken of Matt to my laptop, then packed it all back up. I tipped my head at Humphrey Bogart, who gazed down at me from the vintage posters on the wall of *The Big Sleep* and *The Maltese Falcon*. Then I locked up and headed back to Gary's neighborhood, early enough that I woke up Linda.

"Do you know what time it is?" she mumbled as she opened the front door. "Oh, it's you. Are you trying to piss me off?" she said, leaning against the door and squinting at me. I eyed her pink pajamas with a big red heart on the front of the shirt, wondering if she was trying to draw attention to a certain part of her anatomy.

"I'm sorry, but I need to talk to you. I might know who was here Sunday night."

She perked up a little. "Oh yeah?"

"I've got a photo," I said, pulling out my laptop.

I fiddled with it for a moment as she opened the screen door. I turned so she could look at the screen.

"Is this the guy who was here?"

I showed her the picture I'd taken of Matt standing outside the construction trailer with Gary.

She studied the photo for a moment. "Yeah, I'm pretty sure that's the guy," she said, tapping the screen.

"What?" I glanced at the picture, then back to her, stunned.

"What?" she asked. "That's the guy. He was over here Sunday night."

"Are you sure?"

"I'm positive. The guy here was thin, like that. And he didn't have spiky hair like the other one."

I stared at the picture. She hadn't pointed at Matt, but at Chuck Fitzhugh, the project manager at the Vanguard site where Deuce worked.

Suddenly it fit.

"The company logo, on the side of the truck. You said it looked like circles."

"Yeah."

"Could it have been C's, intertwined together?"

"Huh?"

"Do you have a piece of paper?"

"I guess." She went back to the kitchen and returned with pen and paper.

I exchanged the laptop for the pen and paper, then drew the Criss Cross Construction logo and showed it to her. "Was it like that?"

She nodded. "Yeah, I think that's right. From far away, I thought it was circles." She scrutinized me. "Are you okay? You look like you just saw a ghost." She sucked in a breath, her hand covering her mouth. "Is that the guy who killed Gary?"

"Maybe," I said. I took back the laptop, then slowly backed away. "Thanks. You've been helpful."

CHAPTER TWENTY-FOUR

I couldn't drive to the Vanguard site fast enough. I darted in and out of traffic, and on the way I called Cal.

"What's up?" he asked, sounding groggy.

"It's Chuck Fitzhugh, the project manager. He's the one at Gary's Sunday night." My mouth could barely keep up with my thoughts.

"Huh?"

"I knew I was missing something. How was it that Shane had access to the Vanguard site after hours? He's just a low-level worker, so how does he have keys to get into the site? It's because someone higher up gave him the keys. And how could they take all that stuff without someone knowing? It's because someone *did* know: Fitzhugh. He looks the other way while Matt purchases more materials than they need. Then they sell it off."

"Hey, you woke me up and I can barely think. Can you back up?" Cal asked.

"Sorry." I slowed down and filled him in. "I'm going to talk to Fitzhugh now," I finished.

"Watch your step. If Fitzhugh did kill Gary, who knows what he'll do when he's caught."

"Yeah, I know."

"How does Deuce figure into all this?"

"He must've been a threat," I said. "Although I don't see how."

"You think Fitzhugh will tell you what happened to Deuce?"

"The jig is up, so he's got to."

"What if he murdered Deuce?" Cal asked. "Man, it's going to destroy Ace and Bob."

"I know."

I hung up. The reality that Deuce might be gone was hitting both of us. And what do you say to that?

———

Ten minutes later I parked on the street in front of the Vanguard site. I fed coins into a meter and walked onto the job site. The buzz of saws and pounding hammers cut through the morning air. As I entered the office trailer, the cute secretary smiled up at me. Fitzhugh stood behind his desk in the corner, reading pink telephone messages. He glanced up at me.

"Hey, what can I do for you today?" the secretary asked.

"I need to speak to Chuck," I said, fixing a hard gaze on him.

Fitzhugh cocked his head, a puzzled look on his face. "What do you need?" he asked as he set the papers on the desk and turned around. "Have you found Deuce?"

"No, but I think you know about that. And about Gary," I said. "Quite an operation you have, along with Gary, Shane, and Matt. How'd you get Deuce involved?"

Fitzhugh turned a sickly white as his secretary glanced from him to me.

"I don't know what you're talking about," he said.

"Ah, but you do." I gestured at the secretary, who looked at me, baffled. "You want to discuss this where everyone can hear?"

Fitzhugh swallowed hard. "Karen, can you give us a moment?" he said to her.

She puckered her lips, now appearing a bit miffed. "You want me to leave?"

"Yes," Fitzhugh said. "Why don't you take a break and grab a cup of coffee at Starbucks."

"Uh, sure, Chuck," she said, standing up. "I'll be back in fifteen."

Karen grabbed her purse from under the desk and walked past me, throwing me another bewildered look.

"I'm not sure what you're talking about," Fitzhugh said as the door closed behind her. "It's just a misunderstanding."

I shook my head as I moved into the room. "There's no misunderstanding. I've got you cold. Want to know how?" I leaned against Karen's desk. Fitzhugh stared at me but didn't answer. "I've got pictures of Shane Mundy selling materials to Paxton Electric. Want to bet I can find other companies he's sold stuff to? I have a list of companies from Gary's house. I'll bet they've all been buying discounted materials from Shane and Gary." I paused. Fitzhugh licked his lips but remained silent. "Now where did Shane get all that extra material?" I paused again. Fitzhugh stonewalled. "Okay, I'll tell you what I think. You see, I also know about Matt McClellan and Shane. I've got pictures of Shane taking materials from this job site the other night, and then storing those materials at McClellan Concrete. This is how it goes, and −" I held up my hands, "correct me if I'm wrong − you get Matt, a subcontractor, to purchase more materials than he needs for a particular job. You sign off on the purchases, and Matt and his buddies take the extra materials and sell them –"

"No," Fitzhugh finally found his voice.

"And then you all split the profits."

Fitzhugh shook his head slowly.

"How much are you all making?" I asked. "I'll bet it's a nice little chunk of change. Doesn't hurt when the economy's like it is, right?"

"It's not true," Fitzhugh said.

"I've witnessed it all," I said. "And I also overheard Matt tell Shane that he could set aside some of what he'd stolen to sell on the side."

"No," he said, with less conviction.

"Is that what pushed you over the edge? You found out the guys were skimming off what you took? So you went to Gary's and killed him?"

"I didn't kill him."

"I've witnessed it," I said forcefully. "And I'll bet Matt and Shane will talk. Do you think they won't sell you out to keep from getting in trouble?"

"All right, stop." Fitzhugh held up a hand, defeated. "You're right." He sank into his desk chair and stared at the floor, his elbows resting on his knees. "It's been going on for a while. It didn't start at as much, just a little bit here and there, easy stuff to sell elsewhere. And it was just between Matt and me. Then he got Gary and Shane involved, and we've been making a lot more, overbuying for multiple job sites, then taking the extra and selling it off to other small companies."

"How come you never got caught?"

"We were careful. It's never too much to be noticed, and I approve it all, so no one's the wiser."

"What about the other guys skimming some off?"

He glanced up, anger flashing across his face. "Yeah, that

was stupid. It only complicates things. Too many people involved, and I can't control it anymore. That sets us up to be noticed and caught."

"So on Sunday night you went over to Gary's and you killed him."

"No."

"The next-door neighbor identified you," I said.

Fitzhugh opened his mouth but nothing came out. He hung his head. "I went over there to talk."

"With a gun?"

"Just to talk," he repeated emphatically. "I took the gun because Gary's a hothead, and I wanted him to know I meant business, but that's all. I told him that he was risking the whole operation, and if he didn't stop he'd be out, and he got mad. I pulled the gun on him, just to keep him in check, but he rushed me. And the gun...just...went off. It was an accident."

"An accident?"

His shoulders slumped and his head dipped lower. "I never meant for it to happen," he murmured. "I've got a wife and kids."

I stared at him, vacillating between anger and disgust. The phone rang, loud in the stillness. Fitzhugh didn't move.

"Okay, so you killed him," I finally said. "Then what?"

Fitzhugh looked up at me, his face twisted in anguish. "I've never seen a dead body," he said. I knew the feeling. "I thought about TV shows, and fingerprints, so I used my shirt on the front doorknob, let myself out, ran to my truck, and drove off. I didn't think anyone saw me."

"The neighbor looked out. She described you and the Criss Cross Construction logo on your truck."

He nodded. "Yeah, I figured it was just a matter of time before the police caught up to me." He let out a mirthless laugh. "But I wasn't counting on you."

"I'm underestimated a lot," I said. "You were good, I'll give you that. Acting so cool when I came and talked to you."

"I had to concentrate on the cement pouring so you wouldn't see how nervous I was."

"So...what about Deuce? How does he figure in all this?" I desperately wanted to throttle him so he'd tell me where Deuce was, but I didn't want him to scare him into silence.

"Gary asked him to help out. I think he thought he could get Deuce to help, but pay him a lot less. And because Deuce is..." he shrugged.

"A little slow and a lot naïve?" I said.

He nodded. "Maybe Deuce wouldn't figure it out, and Gary could make more money. I didn't know anything about it until last Friday night. That's when Gary told me that Deuce wanted out and was threatening to say something."

"Did you kill him?" I asked, a heavy, hard knot in the pit of my stomach.

"No!" Fitzhugh shook his head. "Of course not! I think Deuce is a great guy and I was furious that Gary'd gotten him involved. All I did was talk to Deuce."

"Deuce received a call from Gary's phone that night, asking him to go back to B 52's."

"Yeah," Fitzhugh said. "Gary went to the bathroom and I noticed his phone on the coffee table. I called Deuce and asked him to meet me."

"That way nothing could be traced back to you."

"Yeah." Fitzhugh grimaced. "I left Gary's and met Deuce at the bar. We talked and I told him that we'd give everything back and that he didn't need to report us."

"Did he believe you?"

Fitzhugh forced a half-smile. "You know Deuce."

I sighed because I did. "He trusted you all, and you took advantage of him. What'd you do to him?"

"Nothing! After we talked, I went back to my car and Deuce walked away. I assumed he was going home."

"What?" I crossed the room and stared down at him. "You don't know where he is?"

"No! I didn't do anything to him, I swear! He was walking down the street as I drove off." Fitzhugh gave me pleading eyes. "You gotta believe me."

"No, I don't 'gotta believe you'. And unlike Deuce, I *am* going to report you. Maybe the police can get you to talk."

Fitzhugh nodded, all the fight gone. "I know. Go ahead. But I didn't do anything to Deuce."

I pulled out my cell phone and called the police.

CHAPTER TWENTY-FIVE

It didn't take too long for Detective Sarah Spillman and her cohorts, Detectives Moore and Youngfield, to show up. When someone calls to say he has apprehended a murderer, the police tend to move quickly. But if I thought Spillman would greet me as a conquering hero, I was wrong.

"You, wait for me outside," she ordered as she stepped into the trailer. "Spats, get Reed's statement."

Spats looked bored as he pulled out a pen and notepad. "Right this way, sir."

Did I detect sarcasm when he said *sir*? I followed him outside.

"You know the drill," he drawled.

"Can't I wait?" I said. "Spillman's going to come out and I'm going to have to repeat everything."

"Wise guy," he growled.

"I try."

He frowned at me and I gave in, telling him what led me to Fitzhugh. I had to admit, I felt a swelling of pride at what I'd put together, but it died when I said I still didn't know where Deuce was.

"What's going on?" Karen asked as she approached, carrying a Starbucks cup. She nodded at me. "I've been waiting for you to leave."

Spats jerked his head at her. "Who's she?"

"Office manager," I murmured.

Spats went over to her, talking as he guided her to a bench in front of the trailer. He sat her down and walked back to me. Karen stared into space, more puzzled than ever.

As Spats returned, Spillman emerged from the trailer, followed by Moore, who led Fitzhugh in handcuffs to the sedan. By this time, a few construction workers had stopped what they were doing and approached the trailer. It wouldn't take long for the buzz to switch from saws to conversation about the arrest.

"I'll take over," Spillman said to Spats. "Go with Moore. I'll catch up with you later."

Spats handed his notepad to her and walked off.

"So," Spillman appraised me. "The great detective figures out the case."

"If you say so."

Her eyes narrowed and she cocked her head at me, then read through Spats' notes.

"Why do I get the feeling you're not telling us everything?" she said, looking up at me.

Maybe because I left things out, I thought but wisely didn't say. I shrugged.

"What happened to your eye?"

"Bar fight," I said.

She tipped her head up and down, just once, like I'd seen her do before. It seemed to be her way of showing her skepticism. "You just happened to be around Gary's house and you saw Shane, so you decided to follow him, and that led you to

Matt," she glanced at the notepad, "and you observed Shane selling materials to an electrical company, and that led you here."

"No, I thought Matt might've killed Gary, so I asked –"

"Oh, right, the neighbor." Another glance at the notepad. "Linda. And she identified Chuck Fitzhugh as the one who was at Gary's on Sunday night."

"Right. And then I came here and Chuck confessed."

"Just like that," she said.

"Just like that." I smiled at her.

She gazed at me for a few beats. "Uh huh."

"I found Gary's killer, shouldn't that count for something?"

"It does. But we were close. Just needed a little more time."

I shook my head. "Unfortunately I don't have much time."

A hint of softness crossed her face. "I'm sorry about your friend."

"Chuck didn't say anything else to you about Deuce?"

"No. He said he left Deuce at B 52's and doesn't know what happened to him."

"I guess I'm back to square one," I said. A long silence ensued. She reread her notes; I stared at the trailer. "What's going to happen to Chuck?"

"If he can prove it happened like he says, he'll probably get charged with involuntary manslaughter. And he'll face felony charges for the little scheme he had going." Spillman started to walk away, but turned back to me. "Not a bad bit of detective work," she said.

"I didn't find my friend."

"We'll keep looking, too." She paused, then exhaled. "I'm not making any promises, but if you need something, let me know."

"Thanks."

"I've got to go arrest Matt and Shane. How about you stay away?" The gruff demeanor returned.

"You don't have to worry about me," I said. "I've had more than enough of them."

———

It was after noon when I finally left the Vanguard site. To cap off my discouragement at not finding Deuce, I also had a parking ticket. I threw it on the passenger seat, making a mental note to talk to Spillman about it. Maybe she could get it dismissed...after all, I did find Gary's killer.

On the way home, I called Bob and filled him in. He was disappointed and completely distraught about Deuce. I felt like I'd let him and Ace down, but he assured me I'd done all I could. Once home, I fixed a sandwich and ate at the kitchen table, which was unusual for me. I tended to eat in front of the TV, and if nothing good was on, I'd pop in one of my favorite film noir. But I wasn't in the mood for that. I took a few bites of the sandwich, then left it on the plate as I stared out the window. I kept going over everything that happened, trying to find something I might've missed. I finally went downstairs and knocked on the Goofball Brothers' door.

"Reed, hey," Ace said, letting me inside. "What's going on? Bob told me what happened. I was hoping you'd found Deuce. I..." His lower lip quivered.

"I'm trying, buddy," I said. "But I'm coming up empty. I thought I'd go through his stuff again, see if there's something I overlooked."

"Okay, no problem."

He let me in, then followed me into Deuce's room, where I gave it the once-over. As before, I came up with nothing, and stared up at the ceiling in frustration. "What am I missing?"

"I dunno." Ace looked as perplexed as ever.

"How about we look in his truck again?"

"Okay." Ace got the keys and we went outside.

I unlocked the truck and scoured the cab and the truck bed again. Just the same stuff as before. I leaned against the seat and grabbed the papers that had been lying on the floor. "And none of this means anything to you?"

Ace shrugged. "Not really."

I thumbed through them again, noting the list of companies Deuce had scrawled on one of the pieces. I thought about it for a moment, reading the list again and again.

"I wonder..."

"What?" Ace asked.

"I need a computer." I hurried around the side of the building and took the steps two at a time to my condo with Ace at my heels, chattering in confusion.

"Reed, what's going on?"

"This list of companies," I said as I logged onto my computer and connected to the Internet. "T. F. Byers Construction. That's a big company. I've seen their name on some of the major road construction projects around the city. Look at the types of projects they've done: a performing arts center, a high school, office buildings, and a hospital, all over the country. And these other companies, like Pearson," I typed the name into the search engine. "Ah ha! Look, it's a big company as well, building similar projects to Byers." I searched on each company name and they were all large companies who specialized in massive construction projects.

Ace looked at me blankly. "So?"

"Why would Deuce have a list of these kinds of companies in his truck?"

The blank looked remained. "Reed, how would I know?"

"It's a rhetorical question," I said.

"Re-what?"

"Never mind." I stood up and went to my bedroom. I found the list from Gary's house, still in another pair of jeans. I hurried back to the office and sat down, comparing Gary's list to the one Deuce created.

"Look, the list Gary made is of smaller companies where he could sell electrical supplies or rebar – smaller stuff. It's completely different from Deuce's."

"I don't get it," Ace said, scratching his head. "Why would Deuce have a list like this? He couldn't care less about that."

"Does he know people from these other companies?"

"I doubt it." The vacant look on Ace's face remained. "Maybe he was job-hunting."

"You'd know better than anyone if that were true."

Ace shook his head. "No, Deuce loves his job, and he would've told me if he was looking for a new job. I don't why he made that list."

"I don't either," I said. "But it's weird." I turned off the computer and stood up. My mind was racing. "I've got to go. I'll call you later."

Ace stared at me as I rushed out of the office, pulling out my cell phone.

"What's up, Oh Great Detective?" Cal answered. "Did you find Deuce?"

"No, but I need your help with some research."

"Absolutely. Tell me what's going on."

"I need to clear my head. How about I drive up there and I'll fill you in?"

"Sure," he said. "See you when you get here."

"I'm on my way." I hung up and grabbed my keys. "Shut the door behind you," I called over my shoulder to Ace. I bolted down the stairs, leaving him standing in the living room, speechless.

CHAPTER TWENTY-SIX

When I got to Cal's house, and he was just finishing lunch. "You going to tell your mother about the run-in with the dog?" he asked, watching me limp into his kitchen.

I let out a dry laugh. "Yeah, right."

"So, you've got a list of companies you want me to research," Cal said as he took a gallon container of orange juice from his refrigerator and threw it onto a full trash can in the corner. He set the glass he had on the counter.

"Right," I said. "I found the list in Deuce's truck, and they're all big companies, ones that build huge projects."

He gazed at the empty glass, then put it back in the cupboard. "Here, have a soda." He handed me a Coke and took one for himself.

I looked at the orange juice container. At least a glass or two was left in the bottom. I picked it up and shook it. "Do you always throw out good juice?" I said with a smile.

Cal stared at the container. "Oh, it felt empty."

I shook my head. Harvard-smart, but no common sense. "You shouldn't waste it."

"You sound like your mother," he scowled.

"Oh, that's hitting below the belt."

"Come on," Cal said, leaving the kitchen.

I put the orange juice back in the refrigerator and followed Cal back to his office. There weren't any dirty dishes around or a sign of dust. A clean, aerosol smell clung to the air, so he must've just cleaned.

"Let's see what we can find," Cal said as he got comfortable in his chair. "Where's the list?"

I handed it to him as I removed some books from another chair, pulled it over to the desk and sat down. Cal set the list next to his keyboard and started to work, his hands flying across the keyboard.

"Want to do another film noir crossword?" he asked after a moment of me sitting close and watching him.

"No, I'm too tense," I said. "I know I'm onto something."

"Yeah, I can tell." He turned to look at me. "Why don't you move back just a bit and calm down. We'll get this figured out."

I glared at him but moved my chair back. I opened the Coke and took a sip.

"Thank you," Cal said petulantly. He started typing again and I chewed my lower lip nervously.

After what seemed an eternity, he said, "All right. Each company bids on multi-million-dollar projects. Let me look at the executive staff of each."

Again, an eternity went by and I finally decided to lie on the couch. I stretched out, arms behind my head, my right foot twitching nervously.

"Nothing particularly out of order with any of the company presidents, but it'll take more digging to get into their personal finances and backgrounds to know for sure."

Type, type, type. The soft clicking sound of the keys filled the room. I stared at the ceiling and then my eyes closed. I relaxed and was soon asleep.

"Hey, I've got something," Cal said a while later.

I sat up and rubbed my eyes. "I dozed off."

"And snored." Cal grinned. "Forget it. You needed a break."

"What'd you find?"

"It looks like maybe these companies are manipulating the bids."

I got up, sat back in the chair, and stared at the screen. Cal had a number of windows up, each minimized so we could look at all of them at once.

"Manipulating how?"

"Companies can work together to ensure that one of them will submit the winning bid. You can have a bunch of companies bid high and one bids low. They can use some kind of a bid rotation, where each one in turn has the lowest bid. But they usually get caught because you find patterns in how the bids were submitted, or you see alterations to the bids by all the companies but one at the last second. There are countless ways to cheat the system, and you need people who are monitoring this closely to prevent it."

"Doesn't sound like it'd be that easy to do."

"It's not. But see here?" He pointed at one window. "This is T. F. Byers Construction's bid for a power plant in Wyoming." He then gestured at the other windows. "And the bids from the other companies on Deuce's list."

"So?" I said. "T. F. Byers Construction had the lowest bid, so they'd win the project, right?"

"True." He clicked on a document. "I created a list here of the companies on Deuce's list and which ones won the projects they bid on, and the losing bids. This goes back ten years."

I studied the document. "I'm not seeing a pattern."

"Actually, there is, but it's subtle. There are five companies.

For every five or six bids, give or take, each company wins once, but in random order. And somewhere in the mix, another unrelated company or two will win a bid. I think they throw that in so it doesn't look as obvious. When you look at the actual bids, they're doing a number of things to manipulate the bids – like all the companies but one submit an inflated bid, or the losing bids are all close in dollar amount, but higher than the winning bid. And again, at first glance, it's all random. But as I looked at the winning bids over time, each company ends up with about the same amount of profit. So they all make a great deal of money, but it's all done so no one company makes more than the others over time. It's pretty clever how they've done this."

"So you'd need all the CEO's in on this," I said.

"Yep, and probably some others in the companies as well. Certainly some financial people within each company. Which is why I looked into the finances of all the executive staff of each company."

"And?"

Cal cocked an eyebrow and nodded. "Some of them received some pretty nice bonuses, and they all have hefty salaries. Nothing illegal, but there's a lot of money at stake here."

"They manipulate the bids." I processed everything he had told me. "Isn't there a term for that?"

"Uh huh. I found it when I was researching. It's called 'bid rigging'."

"What?"

"Bid rigging."

I slapped my hand on the desk. Cal jumped, startled.

"What was that for?" he griped.

"The other night, Willie was working at Denver Health and she overheard someone from Criss Cross talking about things going on under the table and rigging. I figured they must've been talking about the skimming that Matt and

Gary were doing. And then when we were at B 52's, the night Deuce disappeared, *he* mentioned something to me about rigging, but I thought he was asking me about sailing."

Cal rolled his eyes. "And it took you back to your Harvard days."

I flushed. "Hey, those were good times for me."

"I have to admit, you were a good sailor."

"Lot of good it did me. I completely missed what they were saying."

"Hey, how could you know?"

I continued to mentally chide myself. Did it take me too long to figure this out?

"The bigger question is, how in the hell did Deuce know something about the bid rigging?" Cal asked. "Deuce? Really?"

"He's always wanted to be a detective," I said, shaking my head in disbelief. "How would he know this was going on? You said yourself that it's a complicated scheme."

"Maybe he overhead something."

"That sounds more likely," I said. "However he knew, he got himself into some deep trouble. When we were at the gun range, he talked about needing to protect himself. He must've known he was in some real danger, but I figured he was just kidding around."

"So what happened to him?"

I pondered this. "If Criss Cross is involved in bid rigging, then Lon Carlson, the owner, has to be in on it."

"Yep, he's one."

"He must've known what happened to Deuce when I talked to him."

"Yep," Cal said again.

"He was a good liar." I pondered that for a second. "And knowing Deuce, he told Carlson to stop or he'd call the police,"

I said. I chuckled. "He apparently said the same thing to Chuck."

"That sounds like Deuce."

"So Carlson snatched him. Or had someone do it for him."

"You think they'd kill Deuce?" Cal asked.

I frowned. "And risk a murder charge? I wouldn't think so, but we are talking about a lot of money."

"Millions."

I sat back and stared at the ceiling. "If we don't assume the worst, but say that Deuce is still alive, what would they do with him? You would assume they wouldn't keep him at one of their houses because there's too many people around."

"One of the job sites?" Cal proposed.

"Same thing. Too many people around."

"Unless..." Cal said. "Wait, hold that thought."

He turned back to the computer, fingers flying again.

"What?" I bolted upright and scooted my chair back up to the desk.

"Hold on." More typing. "Maybe..." he muttered.

"What'd you find?"

"Look here." He tapped the screen. "Here's a list of permits. This one here is for an address that isn't on the list of jobs I created. It's a brand new site. And I found records that indicate they're going to break ground next week."

"You don't think..."

"What better place to keep Deuce than a site that no one's at," Cal finished my thought.

"Where is it?"

Cal found it using MapQuest. "Looks like a new medical building, southeast of Castle Rock. Doesn't look like there's too many other buildings or houses in the immediate area. Perfect place to hide someone."

"I better get over there," I said.

CHAPTER TWENTY-SEVEN

The new medical building site was located about ten miles east of Castle Rock, a small but growing town southeast of Denver. Named for a huge, castle-like rock formation on a butte in the center of town, Castle Rock itself is quaint, with family-owned cafés and shops. On my very first case, I'd had to help my client, a *femme fatale* if ever there was one, who was meeting with a nefarious vigilante group. She'd met them in the heart of the town, in the *quaint* part. Unfortunately, the area around the town was a nightmare of crowded roads and cookie-cutter shopping complexes with all the usual stores, and of course, the traffic.

It took me almost two hours to drive from Cal's house in the foothills west of Denver to Castle Rock, and by the time I got there, I was edgy and none too pleased with the snarl of cars on Interstate 25. With each passing second, I worried if Deuce was okay, or if I was even on the right track. If I were wrong, I'd wasted valuable time on this trip.

The sun was setting, painting the western sky in orange and purple hues, as I exited onto Founders Parkway, driving past shops and chain restaurants, and followed the road, which eventually connected with Highway 86. I turned east and kept going, leaving the bustle of town behind.

A few minutes later, I approached the address of the new medical building, but it took a while to find it, as the road leading to the building site was unmarked, and the growing darkness made visibility in the unpopulated area difficult. I finally realized a dirt road I'd passed was the correct place, so I made a U-turn and pulled over.

About a half mile directly down the road, I spotted what looked like a construction trailer, similar to the one at the Vanguard site. I took out my binoculars and canvassed the area around the trailer. No one was around, but the terrain between the trailer and me was hilly, and I couldn't see much. I mulled over my next move. I couldn't drive onto the lot, on the off-chance that someone I didn't want to see might be in the trailer. And if I was in the trailer and someone showed up, they'd know I was there. That left only one option.

I drove down the road and parked in a little turnout, grabbed my lock-picking set and a flashlight from the seat, got out and locked the 4Runner. I tucked the Glock, which I'd remembered to bring, into the small of my back, put the picks in my coat pocket, crossed the road, and struck out across the field. I hadn't walked very far when I heard a car approaching on Highway 86, its headlights cutting into the dimness. I ducked down into a low spot and waited. The car passed without slowing. I stood up and hurried on, picking my way through weeds and low underbrush. Being careful didn't help, and I soon tripped and fell headlong into a tumbleweed. I cursed under my breath as I got up and brushed myself off. The dog bite throbbed and I limped forward.

The trailer finally came into view, a boxy shadow in the gloom, and I stopped and crouched down, taking a moment to catch my breath and listen. Behind me, in the distance, the hum of cars passing down the highway broke the stillness, but none ventured down the dirt road.

I watched the trailer for a few minutes. It was new, with white walls and a large window on either side of the door, each with closed blinds. The Criss Cross Construction logo was emblazoned to the right of the door. After a minute, I was satisfied no one was lurking about. Other than me.

I approached cautiously, staying low, and tiptoed up a set of wooden stairs to the door, cringing as they creaked loudly. I put my hand on the doorknob and turned. Locked. Once again I was forced to pick a lock, but this time I completed the task in seconds. I was getting good at breaking and entering. My mother would be *so* proud. The lock gave and I slowly turned the knob. The door opened outward and I stepped aside, waiting for the flash from a gun muzzle, but none came. I moved inside, standing in the doorway. The last shred of outside light filtered through, and I let my eyes adjust.

It wasn't an office that was being used a lot. There were two metal desks to the left of the door that were pushed up against the wall, waiting to be arranged. Behind them were two large office chairs, pushed into the corner. A few gray file cabinets sat against the back wall. To the right of the door were a water cooler and a small refrigerator, and beyond that was a round conference table and a stack of folding metal chairs leaning against the wall.

I pulled the door shut behind me, and the room plunged into darkness. I pulled a flashlight out of my pocket and was about to turn it on when I heard a noise coming from the right. A bump and that was it. I froze. Was Rosie the Rottweiler's twin sister lurking about? The dull throb in my leg seemed more noticeable.

Nothing happened so I turned on the flashlight. A narrow

channel of light sliced a path in front of me. I hadn't noticed it before, but there was a small door near the conference table. *Must be a bathroom*, I thought. *Was someone in there?* As if to confirm this, I heard the noise again, a muffled thump.

I moved slowly to the door, then stopped in surprise. A folding chair was propped against the door, forced underneath the knob to keep it closed. I'd missed it in the dark. I leaned against the door and listened. Someone, or something, was moving behind it.

My nerves hummed as I worked the chair free, but I held onto it as I opened the door. I wrinkled my nose against a smell of stale sweat and urine. I braced myself for a dog, but instead, I saw Deuce.

CHAPTER TWENTY-EIGHT

He was sitting on the floor, leaning against a tiny cabinet sink, his feet tied up and pressed against a toilet. His hands were tied behind his back, and his head was propped against the cabinet. He was gagged with a rolled handkerchief. He tipped his head up, squinting at the brightness from the flashlight.

"Mm-ff," he said.

"Deuce!" I dropped the chair and the flashlight, got down on my knees and worked the gag free. "Are you okay?"

"Hi, Reed," he rasped. "You found me." He choked back tears.

"It's okay, buddy," I said. "Can you sit up?"

He mumbled something.

"What?"

"Water...hands..." he forced in a scratchy voice.

He leaned forward and I untied his hands and feet. He groaned as he put his hands in his lap.

"Let me get you some water." I stood up, put the flashlight on the table where it shone into the bathroom, and went to the water cooler. Empty. I wrenched open the refrigerator. "Yes!" Bottled water lined the door. I grabbed one, opening it as I hurried back to Deuce.

He took the bottle and greedily drank, his hands shaking, water spilling down his chin. "Oh, that's good," he finally managed a moment later, wiping his face.

"Think you can stand up?"

"Yeah," he said. "My arms and shoulders hurt."

I helped him get up, but he immediately sank onto the toilet.

"Hold on." He stretched his arms for a second, groaning again.

"We've got to get out of here," I said.

"I know, but I'm kinda woozy," he said.

"Okay." I leaned against the door, holding back my impatience. He wasn't in good shape, but with every passing second I wondered if someone would interrupt me mid-rescue.

"How did you find me?" he asked as he held his head in his hands.

I was itching to get us out of there, but it was clear that Deuce needed a few minutes to recover his balance and feeling in his numb limbs.

I gave him the Readers' Digest version, then said, "How did this happen?"

"Gary asked me to help him sell some stuff and he said I could make some extra money. So I took a load of wiring and sold it to Front Range Electrical. I did this a time or two and I made some good money." He stretched again, then continued. "But one time when I went to Gary's, I heard him talking to Shane about stealing more materials. I didn't know they were stealing the stuff. I told Gary it was wrong and that I wanted out. And I said I was going to tell Chuck about it. Then last

Friday night, when Ace and I were walking home, Chuck called and asked if I could meet him back at the bar. I walked back and we talked. He told me he'd stop and return the money, and I said okay, I wouldn't say anything as long as they stopped. Then I started walking home again." He stopped and took another drink.

"Why didn't you tell Ace about what was happening?"

He shrugged. "I was kinda embarrassed. I should've known they were stealing the stuff."

"So they fooled you, don't worry about it," I said. "Think you can walk now?"

Deuce stood up, a hand on the sink to keep his balance. He gave me the water bottle and I set it on the floor outside the door. "Give me a second." He waved a hand in the air in front of his face. "Man, I need a shower." At least he still had his sense of humor. Then a humiliated look crossed his face. "I... wet myself," he whispered. "The first night. I'd had a few beers and I couldn't help it."

"It's all right," I said, growing angrier by the second at what he'd been put through. "Have you had anything to eat?"

He shook his head. "Not much. Someone comes in the morning and again at night. They give me a little water and one day," he thought for a second, "maybe yesterday, the guy had a donut."

"Who was it?"

"I dunno."

I glanced over my shoulder. *If someone came at night...* "Deuce, I know it's hard, but we've got to get out of here."

"I know." Deuce took a couple of steps. "I'm so stiff."

"Come on." I helped him out of the bathroom. "What happened after you left B 52's?"

"I was walking down the street and a big black SUV came

up behind me. Two guys jumped out and before I could run, they grabbed me and threw me in the back of the car. They put a rag on my face and the next thing I knew, I was tied up here." He screwed up his face. "I tried to fight, Reed. I did."

"I know," I said. "They knew what they were doing and you didn't stand a chance."

We made it a few more feet and then Deuce had to lean against the table.

I fretted but tried not to show it. "The guys that took you –"

"He's the president of Criss Cross Construction."

"Lon Carlson."

He nodded. "Yeah, and I think one was an owner of another company in town. Last week I overhead them talking about some bids they had coming up, and the bid rigging. I didn't know what that was, but they saw me and quit talking. Carlson talked to me later and I asked him what bid rigging was. He said it was nothing and I shouldn't say anything about it. He's usually nice, but he was pretty angry with me then. It was kinda strange, so I asked a couple of guys who they were. I went home and Googled them. Turns out all of them were owners of big companies." He looked at me shyly. "I was trying to be a detective, like you." I smiled. "I wrote down the companies, and I was curious, so I looked up bid rigging on the computer. I was trying to ask you about it, but then it was my turn to play pool again." He coughed and wiped a hand over his mouth. "I guess they thought I knew too much."

"You guessed right."

He sucked in a breath, then let it out in a slow hiss. "Okay, I think I can make it."

"Good," I said. I grabbed the flashlight. "We've got to get out of here before someone shows up. Here, put your arm around my shoulder."

172

Deuce did as I instructed and we took two steps.

I stopped. "What's that?"

"A car," Deuce lowered his voice. "They're here to check on me."

My mind raced. "Back in the bathroom!"

"Wait, no! I can't!"

"You just have to. It's okay," I said as I steered him in that direction. "Just act normal and when they leave, I'll get you out of here."

"Normal? I don't normally do this."

Good Lord, I thought. "Act like you have since you've been here."

"Oh, okay."

As the sound of the car engine grew louder, I quickly helped Deuce back onto the floor in the bathroom. I tied his hands and feet and put the gag back on him.

"Don't worry," I whispered. "I'll be right here, I promise."

He nodded but his eyes were filled with fear.

"Remember, act like you have since you've been here."

He nodded again.

I doused the light as muted voices grew louder. I shoved the chair back under the doorknob and in two strides I was across the office. I ducked behind the desks just as the office door opened. I held my breath.

The glow from a powerful flashlight illuminated the center of the trailer, but it left me in deep shadows.

"Let's get him and get out of here," a deep, gravelly voice said.

"You know he can't walk right away," said a second, higher-pitched voice that I recognized. Lon Carlson.

"Well give him a minute, but let's hurry."

"I don't like this," Carlson said. "Murder was never part of the plan."

"I don't like it either," said the deep voice. "But now we've got the cops poking around because of that scam Chuck cooked up, and that detective is still looking for Deuce. We can't keep him here forever, and we can't let him go or he'll go straight to the cops. It's time to get this taken care of. That section of flooring is being poured tomorrow so we put the body in a hole underneath tonight and it's cemented over. No one ever finds the body."

"You are an evil man, Byers," Carlson said.

Byers! Must be from T.F. Byers, one of the construction companies on Deuce's list, I thought.

"Yeah, you'll thank me when you're not in prison," Byers said.

Something scraped, then a thump, and the desk in front of me moved. I jumped. Then I heard the sound of the bathroom door opening. I peeked around the desks.

The folded chair was leaning against the desk, and Carlson and Byers were standing in front of the bathroom door. Carlson held the flashlight, shining it into the bathroom. Byers aimed a gun at Deuce. Deuce squinted as he gazed up at them, but he didn't move. Either he was acting really well or he was too scared to do anything different. Probably the latter. *Pretend like I was never here*, I silently implored Deuce. And then I almost yelped. The water bottle I'd given him was still sitting next to the door! I breathed a noiseless prayer, hoping Deuce's captors wouldn't notice it.

"Let's go," Byers said. He was a big man, with broad shoulders and a bald spot on the back of his head. He reached down and yanked Deuce to his feet. Deuce let out a muffled cry, but he did a good job of acting weak. He leaned against the door-jamb with his eyes closed.

With one hand, Carlson untied the gag, then Deuce's hands and feet. "Don't do anything stupid," he commanded.

Deuce staggered into the room. "Water," he said, making his voice grate.

"You'll get some when we decide," Byers said.

They walked on either side of him, headed for the door. I had to act.

CHAPTER TWENTY-NINE

I stood up and pulled the Glock out. "Stop right there."

Byers and Carlson both jumped and stared in my direction.

"It's the detective!" Carlson yelled.

Byers cursed and aimed his gun at me. "You better be ready to use that."

"Reed!" Deuce hollered as he pitched himself into Byers. The gun went off and I ducked. Deuce and Byers dropped to the floor. Carlson was waving his hands wildly, the flashlight in one hand shining all over like a fast-moving spotlight. I dove to my left as Deuce and Byers wrestled.

I tried for a shot but all I saw in the shadows was arms and legs, so I moved toward Carlson. Then, to my horror, Deuce managed to get to his knees and he had Byers' gun. He pointed it at Byers and Carlson ...and me!

"Deuce, don't!" we all shouted.

He closed his eyes and pulled the trigger.

"Argh!" Carlson dropped the flashlight as his right leg buckled and he dropped to the floor. "He shot me!" The flashlight winked out.

In the commotion that followed, Carlson moaned, Deuce shouted for me, and then a fist knocked me backward. A second later, the trailer door opened and Carlson and Byers dashed outside, Carlson limping as they ran. I darted after them, but tripped over Deuce. He let out an "oof!" and I hit the floor hard, the breath knocked out of me.

When I could breathe again, I scrambled to my feet and hurled myself at the closed door. It budged, but just barely. Apparently, both men were pushing against it from the other side.

"Back off or I shoot through the door," Byers' deep voice boomed from the outside.

I backed up, sucking in deep breaths. "I've got a gun, too."

"Damn, he got me," Carlson moaned. "Ah, it hurts."

"Shut up," Byers said to him. "Hey, Mr. Detective," he called to me. "Throw your gun and cell phone through the window on your right."

My mind raced. Could I fool them and throw out something different? But even in the dark, they'd know if I didn't throw out the Glock. If I could keep from surrendering my phone...I'd been in situations where I didn't have my phone, and not having one stunk. I frantically looked around for something to chuck out instead of my phone. A tape measure lay on the desk. Would that work? Or maybe I should start firing through the door...but Byers seemed to be moving around, and I couldn't pinpoint where he was. Could I hit him?

A loud pop interrupted my thoughts and I jumped. Byers had shot through the door!

"Throw your gun out! Now!"

I rushed to the window, staying off to the side, just in case Byers decided to take another shot at me. I put the safety on the Glock, then reached over, slid the window open, and tossed the gun out.

"Now the phone." Byers' voice came from a different place.

Without thinking, I grabbed the tape measure and hurled it out the window as far as I could, hoping Byers wouldn't notice it wasn't a phone. If I was even luckier, he'd go looking for it.

"You asshole," he said.

I peeked out. In the faint moonlight a shadow moved underneath the window.

"Byers, I've got to go to the hospital," Carlson said, his voice almost a whine.

"We can't," Byers spat at him. He was right below the window, reaching down for the Glock. "How are we going to explain it? They report gunshot wounds."

"We'll make something up," Carlson said, groaning. "I can't just leave this. Oh, I'm feeling lightheaded. I think I'm losing a lot of blood."

I made a snap decision. I grabbed the folded chair leaning against the desk and hefted it up. I peeked back out the window. Byers was right below, still arguing with Carlson. I aimed, then hurled the chair out. It hit Byers squarely on top of his head. He collapsed in a heap.

"Byers!" Carlson yelled. He limped over and shook Byers. Nothing happened. Carlson cursed at me as he rolled Byers over.

I backed away from the window. "Deuce, where are you?" I whispered.

"Over here."

He was backed up against the rear wall, his arms wrapped around his knees.

"I want to go home," he murmured.

Carlson's voice drifted inside. He was threatening to come inside, but the fear in his voice made me think this wouldn't happen. If Deuce and I were going to escape, we had to act quickly.

I put my mouth to his ear. "Are your legs okay?"

He nodded.

"We'll go out the back window and run. Be as quiet as you can."

He nodded again as he pushed himself up.

Out front, Carlson worked to revive Byers, cursing at him and us. I went to the back window by the folding chairs. I grabbed one and opened it, positioning it under the window. I motioned to Deuce. He got up on the chair, hoisted one leg through, then awkwardly pushed his head and torso out. He held onto the window frame, pulled the other leg through and dropped to the ground. I gave him a thumbs-up sign.

I stood up on the chair and climbed out. I was hanging from the ledge, about to drop, when Carlson called through the front window. "What's going on in there?"

I let go and tumbled to the ground.

"Come on!" I pushed Deuce ahead of me and we struck out into the field behind the trailer. It was the opposite direction from the highway, but we needed distance from Carlson.

Behind us, he shouted.

"Oh no," Deuce huffed.

"Keep running," I said. "It's dark and he's hurt."

We went a little farther and stopped. I peered back at the trailer, but didn't see Carlson. I started to the north, wishing we were farther away from the trailer, but knowing that Deuce didn't have a lot of stamina.

"My car's parked on the highway," I said in a low voice. I wanted to stop and call the police, but I didn't want to take the time, and I didn't know if Carlson would be able to see the light from my cell phone. "Stay low and follow me."

"Okay," Deuce whispered.

We slowed our pace, making it easier to move quietly. After a few moments, we were parallel with the trailer. Headlights suddenly split the blackness, and I ducked down, pulling Deuce with me. I glanced toward the trailer. It looked like Carlson was helping Byers into the SUV.

"He's giving up on us," I muttered.

Carlson got into the driver's side and the SUV backed up, then started down the dirt road to the highway.

"Let's go," I said.

Deuce stood up and followed me. As we hurried on, the headlights dimmed and then went out. A few minutes later, we approached the highway.

"There's the 4Runner," I said.

We ran across the road and piled into the car. Deuce let out a huge sigh of relief. I locked the doors, and as I drove off, I glanced over at him, grateful he was all right.

CHAPTER THIRTY

On the way back to Denver, I called Bob and told him I'd found Deuce. I handed the phone to Deuce and he chatted with his brother, his voice breaking at times. He was excited, but mostly exhausted. When they'd finished talking, I took back the phone, called the police, and asked that someone get in touch with Detective Spillman. It took a few minutes and then she called back and I gave her the rundown. She told us to come to the station and give our statements, and her tone left no doubt that I was to follow her orders. As much as I wanted to take Deuce home, I drove to the police station, where Detective Spillman was waiting for us. Once there, Deuce assured us that he didn't need to go to the hospital, so she'd taken him off somewhere to get his statement, and I was brought into another room and left sitting there by myself.

Now I was safely sitting in this room at the police station, contemplating my surroundings. The walls were dull white. There was the table with two chairs, and a video camera mounted up in the corner of the ceiling, and nothing else. And I was having an awful time staying awake. An inauspicious end to finding Deuce. After a while, I propped my elbows on the edge of the table, interlaced my hands, and rested my head on them. I closed my eyes and was on the verge of sleep when the door opened. I sat up and repressed a yawn.

"Are we boring you?" Detective Spillman said as she entered.

"Yes, you are," I shot back. "Am I a suspect?"

She stared down at me. I locked eyes with her. Not the brightest move, maybe, but I just wanted to get Deuce home and go to bed.

Spillman pulled out the chair opposite me, sat down, and slapped a manila folder on the table. "I needed to check your story."

"And it took this long?"

"And we're getting the story from your friend." Her lips curled into the hint of a smile. "Is he really that...naïve?"

I nodded. "It's part of his charm."

She tapped the folder for a moment. "We just picked up Lon Carlson. He's got a gunshot wound to the leg, like you said."

"What did he tell you?"

"He tried to lie, for about a second." She let out a cynical laugh. "He's a businessman, not a professional criminal. He's talking."

"Did he admit what he did to Deuce?"

"Yes, and how Deuce shot him."

"Will you charge Deuce?"

"No, it was self-defense. But there are a lot of legal hoops with a situation like this."

"And then we can go?"

She nodded. "Yes. We're almost finished." She stood up to go. "There's one thing I don't get."

"Yeah?"

"How did you piece all this together? That's a lot of research to get done so quickly."

I tried to maintain a straight face. "I guess I'm good." No way I could tell her about my sidekick.

She gave me a knowing look. "All right," she finally said. "Sit tight for a few more minutes." And she left.

———

'A few minutes' was more like an hour, but eventually she returned and I was able to take Deuce home.

"Deuce!" Ace said as we got out of the car. He ran up and hugged Deuce, grinning and crying at the same time.

"Hey," Deuce said.

Bob hugged him, too, his voice choking as he tried to talk.

Ace was so excited he couldn't complete a sentence. The two Goofball Brothers headed into their condo, but Bob held back.

"I really owe you," he said, holding out his hand.

I shook it. "I wish I could've found him sooner."

A smile spread across his face. "You did fine. Are you okay? Can I get you anything?"

I looked at my watch: three a.m. "Thanks, but I'm beat. I just want a shower and my bed."

"Sure thing. I'll give you a call in a day or two."

"Sounds good."

He hugged me and then followed Ace and Deuce into their condo.

I dragged myself up the stairs.

"Reed?"

I turned around. Deuce was staring up at me.

"What's up?" I said as I trudged back down. "You should be with your brothers."

"I will in a minute. They're just so excited, but I'm tired."
He sat down and stared into space.

"You okay?"

He put his head in his hands and shook his head. "I was
really scared," he mumbled.

I sat down next to him. "I know. I would've been, too."

"But you make it look so easy, being a detective."

"It's not," I said. "It can be dangerous." I thought about how
Willie and I had talked at the hospital. Even though I'd tried to
reassure her, I knew she was right. It was a dangerous job.

"Uh-huh." He looked at me. "Sometimes it's fun helping
you, but...I don't think I want to be a detective anymore."

I nodded. "That's probably a wise choice."

Bob opened the door and looked out at us. "Everything okay?"

"It will be," I said.

Bob hesitated, then disappeared back inside. Deuce and I
sat in silence for a few minutes.

"Why don't you tell them you're tired and you want to sleep
for while. They'll understand."

"Okay." We stood up. Deuce gave me a hug. "Thank you," he
said, then went inside.

I climbed the stairs to my place and did exactly what I said.
I took a long, hot shower, dried off, and crawled into bed. I was
asleep in seconds.

————

Hours later, I stirred when I realized someone was sitting on
the edge of the bed. I yawned, rubbed my eyes and looked up.
Willie was smiling down at me.

"Hey, how'd you get in?" I grinned.

"Cal taught me how to pick locks."

"Really?"

She laughed. "Of course not. Deuce gave me a key."

"I'm glad he did," I said. "Man, I'm tired."

"Maybe I should go home."

"Are you kidding? It's been too long since I've had you to myself." I reached out and pulled her close. "So..."

My cell phone rang.

"Who is that?" she asked.

"Bogie." I said, referring to the ringtone. I stared at the number. "It's my mother."

"You better get it."

"Nah."

"Reed!" She grabbed the phone and handed it to me.

"You're bad!" I mouthed at her.

"It's your mother," she mouthed back.

"Hi, Mom," I answered, stifling another yawn.

"Hello, dear. Are you okay? Did you just get up? It's after ten. You're sleeping late, and you don't sound good. You're not doing drugs, are you?"

"No, Mother," I sighed. "I keep telling you I'm not doing drugs."

"Well, how am I supposed to know? You don't tell me anything and we only see you at holidays."

Okay, she asked for it. "Mother, I'm not doing drugs," I repeated. "I didn't get to bed until three this morning because I was at the police station."

She sucked in a breath. "Were you arrested? What kind of trouble are you in? What am I going to tell your father?"

"I'm not in any trouble. I found Deuce and also got the bad guys. That's what a detective does."

"I know about Deuce because Mrs. Smith called me. Your father and I wanted to say thank you. We're proud of you, dear." Mother giveth. "But I wish you'd choose a better profession. It's so dangerous." And Mother taketh away.

"Yes, being a detective is dangerous," I said. "I've been shot, and beat up, bitten by a dog, and the only drugs I've been on are pain killers. And you have a knack for calling when I'm on pain killers or tired from being up all night working. That's why I sound the way I do."

"Now you're being fresh."

"I give up," I said. "Mother, I love you...can we talk later?"

"I suppose. I love you, too, dear."

I hung up and tossed the phone in the nightstand drawer. Then I pulled Willie into the bed.

"Now, where were we?"

She giggled.

THE END

———

Turn the page for an excerpt from *Out of the Past,* Reed Ferguson mystery book 4!

SNEAK PEEK

Out of the Past, Reed Ferguson Mysteries, book 5

"Put your hands up." The voice snarled, low and menacing. At the same time, I felt something jammed into my back, and I had a pretty good idea what it was.

I was playing pool at B52's, a bar near my condo. I'd just headed down a long hallway that led to the bathrooms, and now this.

"I said 'hands up'," the guy insisted. He leaned in close and I got a whiff of cheap cologne. The gun pushed deeper into my back.

I slowly raised my hands and pressed my palms to the wall, then glanced over my shoulder. " 'Put your hands up'. Isn't that a bit of a cliché?" I asked, stalling for time. There were two of them, one directly behind me with the gun, the other standing off to his right. "You could try something more original, like 'Stick 'em up', or 'Don't move.' Those are good."

A hand grabbed my hair and a second later my head connected with the wall near the bathroom door. My vision clouded with colorful stars.

"Ow!" I groaned. "Was that really necessary?" I resisted the urge to rub my forehead and instead kept my hands to the wall.

"A wise guy," he said.

"Ah, another cliché." I tried to turn around. "Really, gentlemen, you can do better."

He punched me in the kidney. I gasped and slid to the floor, clutching at my lower back. Okay, being a smartass wasn't getting me out of the situation. Why didn't I keep my mouth shut?

"Hey, Oscar, lighten up," the second heavy said in a voice like James Earl Jones as he grabbed Oscar's arm. "The boss is gonna be mad if you rough him up."

I moaned as I turned around and put my head between my knees. "Hey, I just came in to relax, play a little pool." Confusion mixed with the pain. I had to stop and think for a minute... let's see...my name is Reed Ferguson and I'm a private investigator. I love old detective novels and classic movies, particularly film noir, with its dark detectives and femme fatales. But I wasn't working a case now, so why were these guys bothering me?

"I'm not looking for trouble," I mumbled.

"I guess it found you," Oscar said.

Oscar kept setting me up with the clichés, but this time *this* wise guy, namely me, kept his mouth shut.

I sucked in a few deep breaths as I contemplated Oscar's black wingtip Oxfords, then gazed up and surveyed the two men.

Their looks matched their talk – clichéd. Both wore dark three-piece suits and white shirts, thin black ties. Oscar was a white guy built like the Hulk, muscles everywhere that threatened to rip the seams of his jacket. The other was slightly smaller, with skin the color of mocha, and was disproportionately built with a huge chest that tapered into a thin waist and spindly legs. A couple of goons.

Oscar glared down at me. "Feeling better?"

Before I could respond he quickly pocketed the gun as a man in jeans and a green sweater walked around the corner. He glanced at Oscar, then at me on the floor.

"Hey, man, you okay?" he asked me.

"He's fine," Oscar said out of the corner of his mouth. "Leave us alone."

The man shrank away from Oscar, then turned and fled.

I took a few more breaths, working to keep from throwing up. "What do you want?"

The black guy held out a thick hand. "We need you to come with us."

I ignored his hand and edged my way up the wall. The spot where Oscar slugged me was burning. "You could've just asked."

I moved carefully past Oscar and back into the bar. It was eleven o'clock on a Saturday night and B 52's was packed. It was a converted warehouse that was now a pool hall decorated with old plane propellers and advertisements from a time long gone, and I loved hanging out here. The New Wave sounds of the Talking Heads filled the bar, and people jammed into booths and tables in the main room, eating snacks and drinking beer.

I debated running, but I wouldn't get far in the crowd, and I didn't want anyone else to get hurt, so I nixed the idea. I'd ridden over with my friends Ace and Deuce Smith, and they were in the back room playing pool. I wondered how long it would be before the Goofball Brothers realized I hadn't returned from the bathroom. I refer to them affectionately as the Goofball Brothers because they were lighthearted and fun, but a few clowns short of a circus. Which meant I could be gone for a long, long time before they'd notice.

This thought had just raced through my mind when I heard Deuce's lazy drawl.

"Hey, Reed, you leaving?" He was coming from the bar, carrying two mugs of amber beer.

"Uh, yeah, I need to go." I was torn. I could ask Deuce for help, but that might get him snatched with me. And since he was still recovering from a recent kidnapping, I didn't think putting him in harm's way again was a good idea.

I gave a slight nod of my head at the thugs. They weren't my type, socially speaking, and even Deuce should realize that this wasn't a friendly encounter. If he sensed I was in trouble, he could get Natalie Bowman, the regular bartender, to check up on me.

"These guys want to play pool with us?" Ace, the other Goofball Brother, approached.

Yep, a few clowns short. I should've known the brothers wouldn't get it, which was probably best. I didn't need to watch out for them as well.

"I'll see you tomorrow," I said. Even though we didn't have plans, maybe they'd think we did, and come looking for me.

"We don't have any plans tomorrow," Deuce said.

Man, they were killing me.

"Keep moving," Oscar said, nudging me forward.

"See you later," Ace called after us.

The Goofball Brothers were no help, and my girlfriend, Willie, was working the late shift at Denver Health Medical Center, so no one would know until sometime tomorrow that I'd been abducted. Great...

"Can I get my coat?" I asked. I was not only stalling again for time, but I really wanted to get my coat. It was the end of January, and Denver was in what we locals called "Stock Show weather", a bitter cold where the temperature never crawled out of single digits during the week of the National Western Stock Show.

Neither thug answered me, and we kept moving toward the door. I was sandwiched between them as we walked out of the bar. They guided me to a black full-size SUV parked across the street. On my first investigation a few years ago, I'd been similarly forced into a black SUV by guys I wrongly assumed were the FBI. Was this the case again?

"Get in," Oscar ordered me as the black guy trotted around the car to the driver's seat and got in.

I hesitated.

"Relax," Oscar said. "If we wanted to kill you, we already would have."

"Oh, I feel so much better," I muttered as I slid in and Oscar sat down beside me. I was now squeezed between the two, my shoulders curled forward.

"Where are we going?" I tried for cheery, even though my stomach was a knot and my lower back screamed.

"You'll find out soon enough," the black guy said as he started the car. It roared to life and he pulled into traffic, headed south.

"I know his name." I jerked a thumb at Oscar. "What's yours? James Earl Jones? Darth Vader?"

The right side of his mouth twitched.

"It's Tyrone," he finally said.

We drove in silence for a few minutes, weaving our way through downtown Denver. My shoulders began to cramp. I sighed heavily. Oscar turned his head and glared at me. I tried to shrug but couldn't. Tyrone soon turned onto Broadway and we left the high-rises behind. We crossed Colfax and four blocks down, he pulled into a spot on the corner but kept the engine running.

"Now what?" I asked.

"See that over there?" Oscar said. He pointed across the street at a row of large two-story brick buildings.

"Yeah?" I said.

"The brown one, with the neon blue lights," Tyrone clarified.

The building he indicated had two large, recessed windows and an arched doorway. A predominantly college-age crowd lined the sidewalk, waiting to get in. Their attire was somewhat casual, the guys in pants or jeans and dress shirts, a few in tee shirts. The women seemed to be going for provocative, wearing tight jeans or short skirts, and even from my vantage point, the cleavage was obvious. Hardly any of them wore coats, even though it was cold enough to see their breath, but I guess that was the price they paid to be seen and ogled. They all looked to be at least ten years younger than me, and I suddenly felt old.

"Okay, it's a nightclub," I said. "So?"

"That's Vinyl, one of the hottest clubs in SoCo."

I think he was waiting for me to ask what SoCo was, but I knew it meant 'South of Colfax', so instead I said, "Aren't they a little young for you?"

He scowled at me.

"You force me from B 52's to bring me here? What's the deal?" I asked.

"Just wait," Tyrone said, throwing Oscar a look that said 'shut up'.

And so we did. After five minutes of watching young people enter Vinyl, I sighed and exhaled loudly. Five more minutes passed, and I sighed even more dramatically.

Oscar elbowed me. "Knock it off."

"Hey." I grunted and tried to shift away from him, but only succeeded in rubbing shoulders with Tyrone.

"Cool it." Tyrone nodded. "There she is."

Oscar glanced at his watch, then directed his attention across the street. "Right on time."

"There who is?" I asked.

"Her." Tyrone pointed to a woman walking toward Vinyl. "In the pink dress."

'Dress' was generous. The woman wore a one-sleeved mini-dress that looked like it had been painted on, and it barely covered her thighs. She'd pulled her long, highlighted brown hair into a ponytail, exposing tanned shoulders. And even though it was frigid outside, she didn't have a coat. She must've been cold, but she didn't act like it. And she certainly enjoyed the attention, putting more sway in her hips and running a hand through her hair as heads turned. She walked to the front of the line, talked with a bouncer for a moment, then disappeared inside the club.

"Let's go," Tyrone said as he shut off the engine.

They both got out and Oscar leaned a forearm on the hood of the car. He opened his coat so I could see his holstered gun. "No funny business."

I slid out, eyeing them carefully. "What's this all about?"

Both men buttoned their coats, then positioned themselves on either side of me.

"You're about to find out."

Click here to download and keep reading
Out of the Past!

FREE BOOK

Sign up for my newsletter and receive book 1 in the Reed Ferguson mystery series, *This Doesn't Happen in the Movies*, as a welcome gift. You'll also receive another bonus!

Click here to get started:
reneepawlish.com/RFDW

RENÉE'S BOOKSHELF

Reed Ferguson Mysteries:
This Doesn't Happen In The Movies
Reel Estate Rip-Off
The Maltese Felon
Farewell, My Deuce
Out Of The Past
Torch Scene
The Lady Who Sang High
Sweet Smell Of Sucrets
The Third Fan
Back Story
Night of the Hunted
The Postman Always Brings Dice
Road Blocked
Small Town Focus
Nightmare Sally
The Damned Don't Die
Double Iniquity
The Lady Rambles

A Killing
(Spring 2020)

Reed Ferguson Novellas:
Ace in the Hole
Walk Softly, Danger

Reed Ferguson Short Stories:
Elvis And The Sports Card Cheat
A Gun For Hire
Cool Alibi
The Big Steal
The Wrong Woman

Dewey Webb Historical Mystery Series:
Web of Deceit
Murder In Fashion
Secrets and Lies
Honor Among Thieves
Trouble Finds Her
Mob Rule
Murder At Eight

Dewey Webb Short Stories:
Second Chance
Double Cross

Standalone Psychological Suspense:
What's Yours Is Mine
The Girl in the Window

The Sarah Spillman Mystery Short Stories:
Seven for Suicide

Saturday Night Special
Dance of the Macabre

Supernatural Mystery:
Nephilim Genesis of Evil

Short Stories:
Take Five Collection
Codename Richard: A Ghost Story
The Taste of Blood: A Vampire Story

Nonfiction:
The Sallie House: Exposing the Beast Within

CHILDREN'S BOOKS
Middle-grade Historical Fiction:
This War We're In

The Noah Winter Adventure Series:
The Emerald Quest
Dive into Danger
Terror On Lake Huron

ABOUT THE AUTHOR

Renée Pawlish is the author of The Reed Ferguson mystery series, *Nephilim Genesis of Evil*, The Noah Winter adventure series for young adults, *Take Five*, a short story collection that includes a Reed Ferguson mystery, and The *Sallie House: Exposing the Beast Within*, about a haunted house investigation in Kansas.

Renée loves to travel and has visited numerous countries around the world. She has also spent many summer days at her parents' cabin in the hills outside of Boulder, Colorado, which was the inspiration for the setting of Taylor Crossing in her novel *Nephilim*.

Visit Renée at www.reneepawlish.com.

 facebook.com/reneepawlish.author
 twitter.com/ReneePawlish
 instagram.com/reneepawlish_author

Made in the USA
Coppell, TX
29 September 2022

83820778R00121